ELSIE SINGMASTER

WHAT EVERYBODY WANTED

HOUGHTON MIFFLIN COMPANY
Boston and New York
1928

The Riverside Press
CAMBRIDGE · MASSACHUSETTS
PRINTED IN THE U.S.A.

CONTENTS

WHAT EVERYBODY WANTED

I

MARIAN

I

THE organist was concluding her simple and somewhat frightened prelude as Mamma entered the door of the Bon Air Church, followed by Marian and Arietta Lee, Marian, who was the elder, bringing up the rear. The minister saw the advancing procession and delayed by a few seconds his rising to pronounce the invocation, so that Mamma and her train might cease to occupy the eyes and minds of all the assembly. It was a glorious Whitsunday, and the congregation was large. The faculty of the College of Maryland were present almost without exception; the three hundred students were all in their places, perforce; there were also a few persons who seldom attended church, but who had heard of an unexpected addition to the morning service. The minister thought a little bitterly that Mrs. Young would not be Mrs. Young if she did not select this moment to appear.

Mamma, whose maternal title was always accented on the last syllable and never on the first, was well worth the contemplation of this or any other congregation of believers. She had been described many times in her life as 'a glorious beauty' and as 'extraordinarily handsome.' Strangers used the word 'ravishing,' which was outside the vocabulary of Bon Air. Observers were beginning now to speak not so much of her beauty as of how well she kept it, though she did nothing to keep it except to lead an idle life and eat anything she pleased. The aureole of her hair continued thick and golden, her blue eyes neither darkened nor faded, her round cheeks retained their firmness and their ever-arriving, ever-fleeting color, her mouth remained a bow. She had grown extremely stout, but she carried her stoutness with cheerfulness, as though fifty extra pounds made no material difference. She was always cheerful and, she believed, always reasonable. She would have been surprised to know that the minister felt aggrieved; he must be aware that without a car it was difficult for her to get to church promptly.

Her dress was white crape, heavily embroidered in festoons of grapes and leaves. It had been bought at a bargain sale at the shop of 'Louise' in Baltimore, at the cost of a hundred dollars, and it was undoubtedly the most expensive dress which had ever been worn in Bon Air. The sale was not, of course, an open sale to which any one could go, but a private sale for Louise's best customers only. Her hat was a dull white drooping straw with a wreath of corn-flowers and trailing grass. It was a hat which off her head appeared to be twenty years too young, but which on her head suited her exactly. It had been bought at the Hat Shoppe in Baltimore for thirty dollars, and it was undoubtedly the most expensive hat in Bon Air.

Arietta Lee, who was eighteen years old, was taller than her mother and, owing to Spartan dieting induced by fear of growing stout like her mother, as slender and unmodeled as the slenderest boy. She had her mother's blond skin and her mother's golden hair, but her eyes were black and her nose was uptilted. She was pretty now, with the prettiness of youth, and she was also self-conscious and nervous. The college boys were nothing to her, but she did not object to walking between their ranks. Her dress was white organdie, fashioned by Marian, but she had a hat from the Hat Shoppe, not unlike Mamma's except for the wreath, which was made of wild roses. The dress was new and very pretty, but it was, of course, not stunning like Mamma's, and on that account she was vaguely unhappy. She was as desperately in love as it was possible for her to be, and she was unhappy most of the time. The object of her affection was Lucien Clement, a lawyer, a little more than twice her age whom her adoration would have astounded.

An alert rear guard, Marian brought up the procession. She was twenty-one and taller than Lee. She did not in the least resemble Lee and it would have been impossible to find a stronger contrast than that between her and Mamma. Her skin was dark, she carried her head high, there was nothing easy about her. Her dress was last year's white dress, made last year by herself, and altered only by a slight abbreviation of the skirt. Her hat was last summer's white hat, and on it sat a red bird which had done duty on winter before last's hat.

She walked, now with a long step, now with a short, as though she could not easily accommodate her gait to Mamma's slow progress. Mamma liked to saunter down the aisle between the rows of students, Lee tolerated sauntering, but Marian hated it. She hated everything that proceeded slowly, and she had always a fear that arriving at their pew, which was only five from the front, they might find it occupied. It never was occupied, however, and it was probable that any unhappy intruder would rise instantly and depart. Mamma was like a queen in her dignity, composure, and quiet assurance. Of the few little stories which she told over and over, one described the contrasted behavior of Queen Victoria and Queen Eugénie at a royal function.

'Victoria knew the chair would be in place and she sat down unhesitatingly, like a Queen. Eugénie looked behind her to be sure. I hope my daughters will be Victorias.'

The procession was so slow that Marian had time to look admiringly at Mamma and Lee. Bon Air afforded her no congenial companionship, and the young people of her own age found her as dull as she found them. Her family were, along with Lucien Clement, whom secretly she not only hoped, like Lee, but confidently expected to marry, her world, and in them and in her music she lived.

Mamma's hat, she said to herself, was a dream, and so was Lee's. She had time to remember how she had once trimmed a hat for Mamma and how Mamma had wept because it was unbecoming and she could not bear to say so. She could hear Mamma wailing to Lee in the night, 'It breaks my heart to look like a crow, darling!'

Contemplating the hats of Mamma and Lee, she lost a step and was able to take a comfortable stride into the pew. The minister raised his hands, the congregation rose, all bent their heads. She looked up, and a chill passed through her body. It was not the chill of cold, or of alarm; it was the chill of rapture. She clutched the pew in front of her and stood clinging to it, her joyful emotion agitating her spirit as a mighty wind agitates a tree. She forgot Mamma and Lee; they, and Lucien Clement with them, departed; she forgot their clothes, their good looks, everything about them, and let the wind blow through and over her.

The minister stood behind the pulpit, on each side of him huge baskets of peonies. Back of him was the choir, and instead of the usual five persons, the organist and a quartet, there were seven, the additions being a stout, dark-eyed woman, and a tall, red-haired boy. The woman was Ellie Grossart, the

sister of a teacher in the college, and a singer with
the Metropolitan Opera Company in New York.
The boy was Alexander LeConte whose mother
taught in the Bon Air High School and who was
studying the violin in Philadelphia. Mrs. LeConte,
who had two years ago answered the advertisement
of the School Board for a teacher of Latin, had no
connections in Bon Air. She spent her vacations
away from the town, and of her boy little was
known. Could he play? And who had discovered
that he could play? And what happy chance
brought him home now when Ellie Grossart was
here?

Moreover, what a happy chance that it should be
Whitsunday! Marian closed one hand upon the
other — would Madame Grossart, or would she not?
She began to pray — 'God! oh, God, please!' It was
not necessary to say more — the Almighty must
know what had been composed for his glory!

Her prayer had been answered before it was uttered. The organist spread upon the rack an old
volume with the title printed in German, Madame
Grossart stepped forward. The red-haired boy rose
in the shadows behind her and lifted his violin to his
cheek. On his white face, almost lost in the shadows,
showed, near the left corner of his mouth, a pale
birthmark; now merely a pink glow; now, as his
color brightened, a tiny hand; now vanishing as
color surged to his cheek.

Marian clasped her hands more tightly. Sympa-

thy with the organist racked her heart — oh, that all
would go well!

'Millie's scared to death,' she said to herself.
'Simply scared to death!'

She moved her left hand a little toward Arietta
Lee, then drew it back — Lee and Mamma both
laughed at her musical ardor. Her mind traveled
quickly round the church — the minister, the pre-
sident of the college, the townfolk, no one would understand except Dr. Grossart, and she could not possibly catch his eye, since he was doubtless far back,
or perhaps in the gallery. Lucien Clement? — but
thoughts of Lucien were not, in spite of all that she
expected from him, connected with profound dis-
turbances of the soul.

While her thoughts traveled round the church her
eyes were fixed upon Madame Grossart and Alexander LeConte. Baltimore with its many concerts
was only two hours away by bus, but concerts were
expensive, and so, alas! were hats and taxes, and she
heard little music except what she herself created.
She regarded Alexander fiercely, admonishing him
sternly to do well. How presumptuous to accompany
Madame Grossart!

But he was not presumptuous. He moved his bow
— what round and firm and beautiful tone! She felt
a faintness, such as a long-starved person might feel
at sight of a laden table. Madame Grossart opened
her lips. 'My heart, ever faithful, be joyful, sing
praises!' What lightness, what delicacy, what ec-

stasy! She left off singing, Alexander and Millie
together prepared the way for the announcement of
the cause of her delight. The boy steadied Millie,
seemed to steady even the old organ — Bach had,
after all, not nearly so good an organ as this. Madame Grossart told the news she had to tell, trium-
phantly, consolingly, inspiringly — 'Thy Jesus is
here!' How exact, how perfect! It was a wonder that
any one tried to compose anything new. 'Away with
complaining!' — there were probably not a dozen
voices in the United States which could take the first
syllables so powerfully yet so lightly. The organ,
the church, the world, seemed to quicken into life
'Thy Jesus is here!' — final; everything would now
be changed forever in the world. Marian had suddenly religious experience. The minister had not convinced her, the Bible had not really convinced her,
but this declaration convinced beyond question.

The last strain died away, and Madame Grossart
sat down, then the red-haired boy. There was silence, of course, respectful, and to a certain degree
admiring, but only Marian sighed as from a break-
ing heart. Mamma was reading her hymn book; she
would be embarrassed by 'My Heart Ever Faithful.'
She had a few long words which she used, now accurately, now inaccurately, and she was trying to think
of one of these so that she might apply it if necessary
when church was over. The word was 'flamboyant.'
Arietta Lee raised her hand and tapped her lips in
the pretty gesture supposed to hide a yawn.

The minister proceeded quickly with the an-
nouncements. Madame Grossart's singing made him
unhappy with jealousy for the great art of preach-
ing. What were a thousand sermons compared to a
song like that?

Sitting relaxed and exhausted, Marian looked into
a pair of eyes which sought her own. Red-haired
Alexander was tall; though he was back of Madame
Grossart, he could look directly at Marian. She had
never spoken to him and had seen him only a few
times. He was supposed to be very shy, but he
looked at her without embarrassment. Probably he
knew that her father had been a musician and that
she played the piano.

'All right?' asked his fine brown gaze.

'All right!' answered Marian's darker eyes.

II

Marian and Lee stepped out of the pew and
waited, and Mamma led the way down the aisle.
The organist played a stirring postlude, but above it
sentences and fragments of sentences were distinctly
audible. 'Good-morning. A good sermon.' 'A
magnificent voice!' 'I wish she'd sung something a
little less — queer.' 'What was the piece she sang?'
'Good-morning.' 'Or "I Need Thee Every Hour"—
think how that would have rung out!' 'Good-morning, Marian. What did you think of the music?'

Marian's cheeks were aflame, partly because she
was indignant at the loud-voiced stupidity, and

partly because, now that they had reached the door, she could see Lucien Clement waiting at the bottom of the high steps. He stood bareheaded, his cane and his hat in his hand, his thick head of gray hair above all other heads about him. Though he had ample means, he was content to remain in Bon Air practicing law, reading volumes of history which were neither too profound nor too dry, living in bachelor comfort with two deaf servants, and spending an evening or two each week with Mrs. Young and her daughters. He intended from week to week to ask Marian to marry him, but when opportunities came, he was deterred by a cruel recollection. During his law-school days, he had been deeply in love with the daughter of one of his professors and believed that she returned his affection until he overheard a friend teasing her. 'I can't endure him!' she declared in answer. 'He bores me to death, simply to death!' The remembrance was a point of infection, distilling timidity and self-distrust. Marian was sweet, and he believed that she was fond of him, but she was clever and sometimes sharp, and he waited week after week for courage.

At the top of the steps Marian answered her interlocutor. 'The most wonderful music ever heard in this church or this town,' she declared with unnecessary distinctness. 'Surely everybody recognizes the aria from the *Pfingst* Cantata!'

Her speech bred silence in all who heard her, including Mamma. Mamma decided not to use her

word. 'Flamboyant' had slipped away, instead she
had selected 'rococo.'

At this instant history repeated itself. Twenty-
five years ago the sight of Mamma, then Mabel
Daly, coming down the church steps, had held
many students and some townfolk from their dinners. Among the townfolk who paused to enjoy
the sight was Osborne Young, dreamy, belonging to
an old family, interested only in music and poetry
and pictures. To him, Mabel was music and poetry
and pictures.

The sight of Mabel Daly Young, bringing her
daughters down the same steps, had exactly the
same effect. The students were the first out of
church; they stopped by the curb and turned, and
in front of them the townfolk turned also, staring
only a little less frankly. The phalanx was sometimes six deep and as broad as the church and the
narrow yards on each side.

Mamma always came down the center of the
steps. If Marian were not already on one side of her
and Lee on the other, she reached out and gathered
them to her. In the Bon Air Cemetery there was a
memorial to the citizens who had fallen in the Civil
War. In the center stood a gracious and plump
figure, on one side knelt a cavalryman, on the other
an infantryman, and the whole composition reminded Mamma of herself and her daughters.

She liked to pause on the upper step, with the
pillars and gigantic linden trees framing her, and

toss back over her shoulder a word to some one in the rear; or, if no one was there, merely a smile into the middle distance, and then proceed, a hand on the arm of Marian, a hand on the arm of Lee. Her touch was not the grasp of one needing support, it was merely the finger of possession. 'These are mine,' said her hand. There were moments when she shivered, contemplating tall Lee and taller Marian. The years were passing and — she had many vague and unattached quotations floating in her mind — 'And I am not saved,' she said, meaning something very different from the original.

She had never dreamed that she would have a daughter taller than herself before she married again — before, to speak exactly, she married Lucien Clement. The deprivations of her life were many; she had no automobile, she could go to no watering-place, only with the greatest difficulty could she assemble a sufficient wardrobe. Lucien Clement was rich and only five years younger than she.

Usually Marian lent her hand willingly to her mother's light touch, but this morning she unconsciously moved away and her mother's hand dropped. She continued to hear the great voice, now deep and strong, now light and delicate; she heard the strains of the violin, the not-at-all bad support of the organ. She must tell Millie Weed that she did well. She saw Lucien the handsome looking up, with a perfection of feature not often observed in mankind, and a perfection of attire seen only upon him.

MARIAN 13

Catching her eye, he bowed and smiled. Everything
he did was perfect. His gaze left her and passed on
to Mamma, now halfway down the steps. He came
forward to meet them all.

'Good-morning,' said he. He was a man of few
words, and those few not very profound.

Mamma looked up at him — together they were
glorious. Some of those who observed them were
amused, but these were the elderly cynics. Youth
was unanimously admiring.

'Lucien!' Mamma might not have seen Lucien
for a month, when in reality she had seen him last
evening. 'Did you hear the marvelous singing?'

'I did, indeed!'

Mamma's eyes sought the curb. No, Lucien's car,
a long blue roadster, was not there, and her dream of
driving home in its grandeur had to be resigned. It
was resigned only for another dream — she would
walk by Lucien's side, and her daughters would follow after, and the ensemble would be unsurpassable.
She nodded now this way, now that, to townfolk
whom she knew and college folk whom she did not,
and took a step toward home.

'Come, Marian, darling,' she called in her soft
voice. 'We're going.'

Marian was moved by an impulse stronger than
her affection for Lucien, much stronger than her in-
stinct of obedience — one took care of Mamma, but
one did not obey her. A thrilling possibility had oc-
curred to her, so overwhelming that she breathed

heavily. Ignoring Mamma's summons, she entered the side yard and approached the side entrance. Madame Grossart would be apt to go down the aisle, but Alexander LeConte would be apt, if she read his character aright, to come this way. She heard the organ — Millie was, according to her custom, practicing the evening music; she heard footsteps, saw a pair of feet, then a pair of knees, then a long slender body, a pleasant but serious face, and a thick mop of red hair.

'Mr. LeConte.'

Alexander LeConte stopped short. In one hand he carried a music case, in the other a violin. He flushed scarlet; the flood receding left a few freckles showing plainly, then returning covered them once more. On his cheek near the corner of his mouth, the birthmark showed plainly.

'Don't call me that!' he commanded in a tone which was at once pleased and positive. 'My name's Alexander.'

'All right!' laughed Marian. 'Alexander.'

'Or Alec.'

'All right — Alec,' agreed Marian. 'I'm Marian Young. I would like' — the intensity of her desire and the eagerness of his gaze confused her — 'I mean how long are you going to be in town?'

'A few weeks.'

'I've played the piano almost all my life and I can read easily,' explained Marian, her words hastening one after the other. 'I thought you might like to do some practicing and I could accompany you. You play beautifully. It would be a treat and the greatest benefit to me. But don't do it unless it would help you.'

The crimson flush receded and the freckles and the pale hand appeared, then were covered once more.

'I've heard you play. I've walked up and down outside your fence listening.'

'Mercy!' cried Marian.

'You'd have no trouble accompanying me, none whatever.'

They walked side by side toward the pavement. Mrs. Young and Lee having vanished, the throng had hastened dinnerward. Only a single figure remained, that of a little woman who paced slowly back and forth, not impatiently, but as though waiting had its own pleasures. When Marian and Alec came out the gate, she was directly before them. One noticed first·her eyes, glowing and dark, the sign of an ardent spirit, then her somewhat pale and tired face, the evidence of a life of anxiety and labor. She smiled as they approached.

'Mother, this is Miss Marian Young,' announced Alec easily. 'She's invited me to play with her while I'm at home, or rather she's offered to play accompaniments for me.' Alec was both calm and excited, calm as far as the social amenities were concerned, excited in a deeper stratum.

'How delightful for Alec!' answered Mrs. Le-

Conte, who also was at ease. 'You mustn't let him work you too hard. He's insatiable.'

'So am I,' declared Marian. 'I'm very glad to know you, Mrs. LeConte. I was out of the High School before you came here. I hope I'll see you often — I must run after my mother, she'll think I'm lost.'

'Have you agreed upon a time?'

'That we forgot!' laughed Marian. 'Would this evening be too soon?' She remembered Lucien — Lucien came always on Sunday evenings. 'The early evening, I mean. Then in the mornings, except Thursdays and Fridays when I give lessons. On those days it would have to be in the afternoon.'

'Any hour will suit me.'

Mrs. LeConte laid her hand on her son's arm. 'Whoever plays with him must be cicerone and time-keeper and business manager. He may appear at midnight or at three in the morning, if he has a problem to solve. There are rewards for his acquaintance, but there are penalties as well. Don't let him abuse good nature.'

'I won't,' promised Marian. 'Good-morning. Seven o-clock, let's say.'

III

Marian hurried down the empty street. Heavenly! She must practice all afternoon. But they slept, they always slept on Sundays, and on week days too for that matter, and to rouse a sleeper in the Young household with music was a cause for seriously hurt feelings. She took the corner on a trot and could see far in the distance three figures, Mamma and Lucien and Lee. She began to run lightly as a deer down the tree-arched street, hoping that she could cover a good distance before Mamma looked round and was horrified. It was necessary that she get home promptly because of Celeste Imogene, the maid, who was that afternoon to submit to an annual baptism in the creek and must be away immediately after dinner. The other members of the family could do little with Celeste, and there was no telling how she might show her resentment if they were late on the important day. Marian traversed a block, another, then she stopped running and took a normal pace. Young and in abounding health, she was not in the least winded.

Directly before her Lucien walked with his hat in his hand, his iron-gray head uncovered. Mamma said that he would never lose his hair; if men kept their hair till they were thirty-five it was theirs forever. It was delightful to walk thus behind Lucien and contemplate him. He was her property. She had once heard, coming down the steps of the church, a question — 'Which onc'll hc take?' The tone was hateful and the answer was a laugh. How absurd! — Mamma was too old, Lee was too young. She put the insulting question out of her mind so successfully that she did not think of it now when Lucien walked with Mamma and Lee.

The three reached the gate and Lucien was lifting his hat when a car drove to the curb. Lucien would certainly not be invited to dinner on this nervous day! He was seldom invited to a meal; the Youngs had meals with him much oftener than he with them. They seldom entertained except at large afternoon card-parties at which Mamma and Lee paid back favors of long standing. Mamma often said laughingly that there was no reason to feed the gentlemen; so long as they were allowed to come, they were pleased with lemonade.

Marian thought, seeing the car stop, that Lucien had had his roadster driven thither for him. But this was a limousine, not a roadster. Lucien had absolutely the best car for a conservative bachelor with plenty of money; the car at the curb was the best car for the richest man in the world, or for a king. At the instant that Marian joined her mother and sister and Lucien, a gentleman stepped out. There were two other men, one of whom had opened the door.

'Who can it be?' Marian asked herself.

'Chauffeur and footman!' Mamma spoke in an astonished whisper to the world at large.

Lee said nothing. She entered the gate like a pettish child and walked up the path. When she had what Mamma called a spell, there was nothing to do but let her get over it and take no notice meanwhile.

The gentleman who stepped out of the back of the car was tall, as tall as Lucien and much broader. He had a pointed black beard and fine teeth which he showed in a smile. He came forward, his hat in his right hand. His left arm, limp against his side, had an appearance of impotence. He brought with him an aroma of fine tobacco and delicate scent which suggested riches and power. One searched one's mind — at least Marian and Lucien searched their minds, to find the source of a vague suspicion. When he spoke, his rich voice told what it was. His eyes were on Mamma, and he seemed to grow a little pale at sight of her, which was not strange. She was incredibly lovely as she stood in the brick gateway with its white urns far above her head, the blue cornflowers in her hat repeating the blue of her eyes. She looked as though she defended that which was back of her, which was proper; and as though she would give way instantly at the right word, rightly spoken, which was gracious and hospitable.

The eyes of the stranger gazed into her blue eyes, then over her head at what was beyond her, then back at her. That which was beyond her was in its way as lovely as Mamma, an old brick house with tall white pillars and about forty ancient oak trees on each side. A brick walk led in from the gateway, and up this walk went Lee in her short ruffled white dress as though she were the fairy chatelaine. From out the door looked a black face above a white apron, irate when seen close at hand, but at this distance fitting into the picture.

The pictorial quality of her house — it was really

her own house, willed to her — suggested to Marian the business of the visitor. Bon Air had been saved from the ravishing of antique hunters by the fact that it was off the general line of travel, but a few explorers had appeared during the spring, and it was probable that like Herculaneum it would be compelled at last to give up some of its treasures.

'My dear madame' — the stranger spoke in a rich tone, with a slight trilling of the *r*. 'Please do not banish me until you hear my cause.'

Mamma smiled — she would not banish any handsome gentleman, least of all one who came in a limousine of foreign manufacture.

'I've driven past your house several times, but I didn't like to approach unintroduced, and I've never until this moment seen any one to whom I might express my admiration and beg that I might stand at gaze. My name is Henry Obenchain.'

Mamma's cheeks grew pinker as though she saw some enchanting sight. 'Of Baltimore?' she inquired in most mellifluous tones.

'Yes, madame.' Mr. Obenchain bowed as though she had asked, 'From the Court of St. James's?'

'Of the firm of Obenchain and Borleis?' Mamma's cheeks took on a still brighter pink; what she saw was an eight-story building, occupying a block, filled with silks and satins and jewels, and high-heeled slippers and evening dresses and fur coats. It was also filled with kitchen utensils and furniture, but she was not interested in furniture; she, or rather

Marian, which was the same thing, had an ample
supply. She was about to say pleasantly, 'You have
been my creditor at times,' but she caught herself.
Messrs. Obenchain and Borleis were her creditors
now and it was best to avoid the subject.

'So you like our little house?' she asked instead.

'It is the only perfect house I've ever seen, and
not, I should say, a very small one.'

'This is my daughter, Miss Young,' said Mamma.
'This is my younger daughter, Arietta Lee — why,
she's gone!' Mamma laughed her rippling laugh.
'Gone! This is our friend, Mr. Clement.'

Obenchain's bow to Marian was deep, his hand
extended to Lucien, cordial. To Mamma he said the
obvious thing — 'Not your daughter, surely!'

'Yes.' Mamma did not object to obviousness
when it was admiring. 'It's this droopy, flowery hat,
selected by my daughter' — she intended to pause
here, but some telepathic admonition bade her continue until she had told the whole truth — 'my
daughter, Arietta Lee.'

Obenchain's eyes swept across her and her hat to
the house beyond. Marian quivered with alarm.
Again the head of Celeste was thrust from the door,
wearing now not the white cap of ceremony but a
bright red rubber bathing-cap, a part of the costume
provided for her immersion. Was it merely a danger
signal, or was she preparing to leave with the dinner
unserved? Surely Mamma would not invite this
stranger in!

This was exactly what Mamma proceeded to do. 'Perhaps you'll come in and look about?' said she. 'We have some poor old chairs and tables and bric-à-brac — they are even older than the house.'

'I'm sure you have priceless things,' answered Obenchain. Either he had a modicum of sense, or to his mind penetrated a message from the brain of this tall, slender young woman with the red bird in her hat. Her hat was becoming, but it was not stylish like the hat of her mother. He would have liked to give her a hat. 'But I'll not stop now. Another time, if I may.'

'You may indeed!' Mamma laid her hand on Marian's arm. 'Good-morning, sir. Good-morning, Lucien.'

Mamma swept up the walk; though her skirt was short, she could sweep. From the brick paved terrace she looked back, a glorious white pillar on each side of her. Obenchain and Lucien were talking, and presently Lucien stepped into the beautiful car. Obenchain still held his arm to his side.

'That might make a pleasant friend for Lucien.' Mamma spoke dreamily; her mind had already traveled to the moment when these two gentlemen should contend for her hand. Life, empty enough in the early morning, empty enough when church was over and her audience gone, was suddenly very rich and deep.

But life became in an instant both meaningless and shallow. The nostrils of Mamma and Marian,

and it must be also the nostrils of Lee, were assailed
by an odor, sharp and acrid, the most unpleasant
and unhappy odor in the world to assail nostrils just
before dinner.

'She's burned the beans!' cried Marian.

'She's burned the fowl,' wailed Mamma.

Together they stepped into the spacious hall. On
one side two doors opened into a drawing-room, on
the other a door opened into a sitting-room and another into a library. The poor old chairs and tables
were, as Obenchain guessed, priceless in value, rich
in beauty, and many in number. There were also
sofas and pictures and desks and objects of glass and
china. Through the Palladian window at the turn of
the stairs one could look into the boughs of the oak
trees. Stepping down the stairs, her hat discarded,
disgust on her pretty face, came Lee.

'What hasn't she burned?' she demanded with
shrill scorn.

Marian walked swiftly through the hall, past a
low sofa with arms like the necks of swans, past a
table which had carved feet tipped with brass and
which bore on its shining surface and against its
upturned leaf a pair of hurricane lamps with engraved shades, into a dining-room. Here also was
superb furniture, but she saw only a tall girl of ebony
complexion placing dinner on the table. Her apron
had been removed, her dress was purple, and she
wore the scarlet cap. It was in design a liberty cap
and its position over one ear symbolized that lauded
state which gave it its name.

'Celeste,' said Marian, 'I wish you to leave this house instantly.'

Celeste looked up. If Mrs. Young or Lee had ordered her to leave, it would have been a gesture merely, but Miss Marian's word was law because Miss Marian paid her. She was alarmed; nowhere else would she have the easy position which she had here.

'Think of any one who's about to be baptized losing her temper because people are unavoidably detained! What good will baptism do you, Celeste? Tell me that!' Marian waited for no answer; Celeste needed baptism as a peevish child needs a whipping, and the sooner she went through the rite, the better. 'Go down to your cabin and pray the Lord to forgive you.'

Celeste began to cry. 'I ain't got nothin' 'gainst you, Miss Marian. I just didn't know was she goin' to invite two men to dinnah, an' I —— '

'So therefore you burned the dinner — that was certainly sensible.' Marian took off her hat and walked toward Celeste with the air of one shooing a chicken. 'Go on! You can't do anything properly now. You're not even dressed to wait on table.'

Celeste retreated into the pantry, into the kitchen. There she looked upon a scene of disorder. Upon it Marian looked also.

'Do as I tell you!'

Marian returned to the dining-room. Mamma and Lee were standing looking at the dinner.

'There are edible portions, I'm sure,' said Mamma, hopefully. 'It's just as well that Mr. Obenchain didn't accept my invitation to come in.'

Lee slipped into her chair. 'Mister who?'

'That was Mr. Obenchain, of the firm of Obenchain and Borleis. You've certainly heard of them, my dear!' Mamma's tone was not sarcastic, but sweet. 'Yes? He admired this house and stopped to say so. He's coming again. I think I shall invite him to dinner probably. I wonder whether our Lucien would shine in such company?'

Marian turned and looked at Mamma, her face aflame. 'Lucien would shine in any company,' she declared hotly.

Lee turned and looked sidewise at Marian, on her pretty face a strange, unhappy expression, as though she saw in Marian an enemy.

'Lucien,' said Mamma lightly, and using an entirely new word, 'is a little provincial. Now let us eat. Where is Celeste?'

'I sent her off,' explained Marian. 'She'll get baptized, then she'll behave herself. I'll clear the things away.'

'Oh, my darling!' protested Mamma. 'On this hot day! And Sunday! So many burdens fall on you!'

Lee spoke hotly and ill-temperedly, albeit truthfully. 'Marian likes it! She has a fine character and she enjoys showing it.'

'Now! now!' reproved Mamma gently. She bent

her head. She could remember at this moment only
a very short grace, and she prolonged it unctuously.
'God — bless — this — food, A — men.'

IV

Marian stood perfectly still in the dining-room
listening. Before her was the dining-table with a
pedestal and carved feet tipped with brass, like the
pedestal and feet of the table in the hall. Its top
bore only empty dessert plates, finger-bowls, and a
center-piece of flowers; it was not as Celeste left it,
littered with pepper and salt cups and débris from
earlier courses.

Marian was listening for sounds from above, her
head cocked. Mamma's room was thickly carpeted
and her footsteps could not be heard, but the creak
of her beautiful century-old day-bed could be heard.
There was no carpet on Lee's room and from there
sounded a high-heeled tapping. On the table beside
Mamma's day-bed were fashion magazines, and an
old-fashioned novel — she was as up to the times in
one taste as she was behind the times in the other,
and also a box of chocolate candy, her beautiful complexion notwithstanding.

It was hard to tell what was beside Lee's bed.
Lee closed her door tight to Marian; she was secre-
tive, difficult, hard to please. She was also distress-
ingly idle. Sometimes she made her bed, oftener she
did not. Sometimes she played light, foolish tunes
like 'Marchèta' and 'Valencia' and 'Souvenir' on

Marian's piano, sometimes she did not touch the piano for days. She had some facility, but her taste was execrable. Marian did not protest; saccharine as the tunes were to the ear of a classicist, she was glad when Lee played.

She heard at last the creak of Mamma's day-bed and the dropping of Lee's high-heeled slippers, and with a sigh of relief and a deliberate, purposeful step, she proceeded with her work. Now that they were asleep, she could expect their eventual waking. She had taken off her dress and put on an apron which covered her, all but her slender, muscular arms. She cleared the table, brushed the rug, mopped the edges of the floor, bowed the shutters, and entering the kitchen closed the door behind her. Next to playing the piano she liked bringing order out of chaos. If she could play the piano at this moment, chaos might await the return of Celeste, repentant, and for the next month amiable and industrious. But she could not play the piano until the day-bed creaked again and Lee's heels began to tap the floor.

She walked to the door and looked out. Back of the house, as on the sides, were oak trees with a thick span of mighty trunk and a broad reach of spreading arms. She felt the rapture of possession — these trees were hers and she would never give them up. The property had been willed to her father and entailed upon his oldest child by a maiden great-aunt. To Osborne Young, upon whom arthritis had set its cruel grasp before youth was over, it had been salvation. His malady began fortunately, if so happy a word could be used in connection with so serious an affliction, in his ankles, and proceeded with slowness which made him hope for a long time that it might be cured. His dextrous and powerful hands were the last part of his body to stiffen except his heart.

He had been Marian's only teacher, and his instruction had a thoroughness which her mother thought cruel. Before he died he gave Marian brief counsel. 'This house is yours to do what you like with. If I know you, you'll never wish to part with it. If it should become necessary to sell it, the furniture will bring a large sum. If you three stay here, your combined incomes should be sufficient, and you can add to yours by teaching the piano.

'If you marry — that will be different. But keep this dear house if you can; it will comfort you whatever happens to you. Lee will probably marry early.' Of the other member of the family he spoke after a pause. 'Your mother may marry also.' It was the only remark of her father's which lacked wisdom — mothers did not marry! The mere thought made her blush. Her mind persisted at times in dwelling upon the intimacies of marriage until she bade it sternly to abstain. It was impossible to think of Mamma marrying.

'Remember to stand up for yourself!' her father charged her finally.

A wind blew under the trees; the morning had

been warm, but the air was changing and the evening would be cool enough for hearth fires. When she had finished the dishes, she brushed up the hearths in the dining-room and sitting-room and drawing-room and brought in paper and kindling and oak wood.

On the drawing-room walls were Sully portraits; on the floor was an ancient rug, magnificent and happily indestructible. Here were other pieces of fine furniture, and here, best of all, was the grand piano, her father's last purchase. She thought of Alexander LeConte's violin; she would handle it and get him to show her something of the first positions. There should be flowers, here and in the sitting-room. She ran out to the small flower garden in a sunny space at the back of the house and gathered sprays of delphinium and valerian and arranged them in tall vases. She moved faster and faster — if she was to be perfectly free and have an unperturbed spirit, she must make sandwiches and salad for supper.

The afternoon light was changing, and she welcomed the early evening when the sun pierced the gloom under the trees in long horizontal bars and the falling dew brought woodland scents into the house. What would they play? There were a thousand compositions for piano and violin that she had never heard. She knew only popular things, banal from repetition on the Victrola. She took from a shelf in the library 'Lives' of Bach and Mendelssohn and

Beethoven and looked through the lists of violin music. She read their names aloud — concerto and sonata, romance and mazurka.

Her eyes, lifted from her book, fell upon Lucien's photograph, standing framed on her mother's desk in the sitting-room. Perhaps he would come while they were playing. They would finish the composition, then she would make it clear to Alexander that he must go. She held Lucien's picture to her cheek. This evening, if she could see him alone, he might ask her to marry him.

She walked about an immaculate drawing-room, she looked out under the oak trees. Her heart beat rapidly; she believed that it was in ardent love for Lucien.

'Mr. Obenchain would absolutely and entirely lose his mind if he saw the inside of this house,' she thought. 'Surely he couldn't have expected to buy anything!'

She sat down on the piano bench. It was now four o'clock and the waking of Mamma and Lee was due. They had slept two mortal hours. What punishment to sleep two mortal hours on a spring afternoon! The minute they woke she would begin — Chopin, Opus 10, Number 1, played twice to loosen her wrists; Beethoven, the Scherzo from Opus 2, Number 3, twice to lighten her touch; then Bach, the Fantasie in C minor, to rejoice her soul; then nothing else till Alec came.

In the dining-room she listened, her head again

cocked slightly. There was no creaking of the day-
bed, no tapping of heels. Sometimes when their
naps were over, Mamma and Lee held a rendezvous,
Lee sitting upon the bed of Mamma, or Mamma
lying upon the bed of Lee. What they talked about
was clothes. Ah, they were talking now!

Returning to the drawing-room and closing the
doors behind her, she struck a heavy chord. She
would play well, she would astonish Alexander. Up
and down, up and down raced her hands, long, lean,
accurate.

She looked up at last. The door had opened; enchanting in light blue crêpe de chine, Mamma stood
by the piano.

'Are we to have nothing to eat?' she wailed as
though she were starved. But Mamma was anything but starved.

Marian looked at the clock and sprang up. She it
was who wound the clocks and they were always
right.

'Six o'clock! Gracious! I was going to play no
more than an hour. Everything's ready. Come
along.'

Mamma looked across the polished table and the
sandwiches and salad and iced-tea, first at one
daughter, then at the other.

'What are my girls going to do this evening?'

Mamma really wished to know. She had been
studying her reflection in the glass — time was passing. She must bring things to a head with Lucien.

Lucien could give her everything she wanted, freedom from anxiety which harassed her, plenty in
every sense of the word. Sometimes she thought of
sitting down beside him and laying her beautiful
head on his shoulder and shedding a few tears, but
even she had principles of behavior. Could she have
but known, such behavior would have won lonely
and humble-minded Lucien instantly.

'I'm going to play violin music with Alexander
LeConte,' announced Marian.

'That will be nice. Please keep the doors shut.
And my little girl?'

'I don't know what I'll do.' Lee saw herself sitting
the long evening through with Mamma and Lucien,
praying that Mamma would leave. Old, old Mamma!
Sometimes Lee counted her fingers, or objects round
the room, or the ticks of the clock. If Mamma would
only go to bed where old ladies of forty-five belonged! But she never went to bed. 'Except in day-
time,' Lee sometimes said meanly.

'Why not visit Nellie Roper?' Mamma spoke
easily, as though there were no hidden purpose under
her suggestion. 'Her young man's away.'

'I don't know that he's her young man.' The
happiness of others offended Lee, since she saw no
prospect of being happy herself. Nellie Roper was
no older than she and very homely — it was unthinkable that Nellie should have a devoted lover!
She might, she believed, capture Nellie's lover, or
win any one of fifty college boys, but she had no

interest in boys. Boys were awkward, dull, unfinished.

'It's quarter to seven,' announced Mamma idly. What was in the back of her mind was that Lucien Clement would not come till eight.

'Why, so it is!' Marian sprang up. 'Do you mind if I carry out these plates? That boy will be here at seven. He's to be in town for several weeks and we're going to play every day.'

Mamma sighed. Her eyes met Lee's; in this matter they were agreed — Marian's music was the heavy burden of their lives. Suddenly Lee lifted her head; she spoke explosively from irritation long endured.

'Marian Young, do you know that you mutter when you play?'

'Do I?' laughed Marian. 'I'll stop it.'

'I suppose it's called counting,' said Mamma, who stood in dread of strife.

'It's not counting either,' contradicted Lee. 'I can stand counting. It's mumbling and grunting like a pig.'

Again Marian laughed. 'Believe me, I don't want to mumble and grunt like a pig! Roar at me if you hear it again, will you? Or come and slam the door. As for playing' — Marian looked at Lee, at Mamma pleasantly but firmly — 'the playing must go on. It helps to earn our living.'

V

Marian sat down at the piano as the clock struck seven. She spread out her hands and began again the sweeping arpeggios of Opus 10, Number 1. Her mind dwelt upon the ancient trees, the white pillars, the gateway with its urns, the lingering light, the flames of the candles glowing in their globes of engraved glass, the portraits of departed Youngs. The music made the moment perfect — Alexander Le-Conte would be thrilled as he came up the brick walk.

Mamma sat in the sitting-room at her desk. She had no correspondents except tradespeople, but sometimes she wrote notes to Lucien which she afterwards destroyed. They began, 'Dear Lucien'; or, sometimes, 'Dearest Lucien'; or, 'Dear, dear Lucien.' She seldom got beyond the affectionate salutation and she tore them all into fine pieces and put them into the waste-paper basket.

She had at this lovely moment no sense of general well-being as Marian had, nor did the proximity of beautiful objects make her happy. She longed for Lucien to arrive — perhaps this evening he would reach the point which she believed he had long been approaching. If he came, she could forget that to-morrow was the first of the month and that tradespeople would ask, or even demand, their money. She opened the drawer of the old secretary and took out a pack of cards and a little board and sat down in the low armchair which was her favorite, and began to play solitaire, listening, meanwhile, with the larger part of her mind.

Lee had gone to see Nellie Roper who lived directly across the street where the houses were set near to the pavement. She insisted upon sitting on the porch from which they could see her own gate and she meant, when she saw Lucien's tall figure, to run across and accost him. There was something terrible in the thought of Lucien and Mamma together — old, old Mamma! There was something equally unpleasant in the thought of Lucien and Marian. Marian was a poky high-brow; she cared only for stupid books and for her music, she could have no possible idea of love. All that Lee asked was to be taken care of and made much of, and Lucien would take care of her and make much of her as he always had. She determined that she would seize his arm and beg him to stay out with her in the moonlight, but when the time came she would do nothing of the kind. She was afraid of shocking him and she wished above everything to stand well in his eyes.

Marian had played through her arpeggios only once when she heard Alec at the door and went to meet him. He stood tall and straight, his violin case in one hand, his music in the other. The last rays of the sun, shining horizontally through the western windows, as though the day were returning, dimmed the candle-light and illuminated his red hair and his face which was pale with excitement and anticipation,

and upon which every freckle and the rosy mark
showed plainly.

'You see I believed you!'

'You'd better believe me!' Possessed by excitement, Marian almost seized him and drew him directly to the piano; instead, having a proper sense of
respect, she led him into the sitting-room. Trans-
porting melodies sounded in her brain, deep chords,
delicate tappings, trills light as bird songs.

'Mamma, here's Alexander LeConte.'

'Good-evening, Mr. LeConte.' Mamma made a
difference between the classes of society; though the
stratum from which she sprang was far beneath that
of the LeContes, she did not lay down her cards or
put out her hand. But her smile was bewitching. 'I
hope you don't think me wicked!'

'Not at all!' protested Alec.

'We'll begin instantly,' said Marian. 'Mamma,
do you wish me to close the doors?'

'If you please,' answered Mamma. 'It isn't that I
don't enjoy music, Mr. LeConte. But practicing —
that's different.'

'Yes,' agreed Alec. 'I always have as much mercy
as I can.'

'I'll see you before you go,' promised Mamma
graciously.

Marian led the way to the drawing-room. A fire
burned in the grate, a shaded lamp by the piano illuminated the large cluster of delphiniums and valerian on a table near by.

'Ah!' sighed Alec.

'The flowers, you mean?' Marian had closed the door from the sitting-room into the hall, she was now closing both doors from the hall into the drawing-room. She lifted the windows toward the side street — the fire was not exactly necessary. Mamma rose softly and opened the door from the sitting-room into the hall — oh, stupid young Marian, who knew nothing of the nerve-racking yet delicious pleasure of waiting!

'I mean everything,' explained Alec.

Marian sat down at the piano. She had never spoken to Alec before to-day and had seen him only once, but she took no pains to make him feel at home. Neither uttered the polite sentences of new acquaintances. They were members of an assembling orchestra, the thing to do was to play. It was like being introduced by a third person who was a close friend to each; it was even better than that — such friendships are proverbially uncertain.

'Tuned last Monday,' said Marian. 'Lucky!'

Alec laid out his bow, tightened a key, touched a string with his finger, tightened another string, played an arpeggio lightly.

'Tuned this minute,' said he. He placed a volume before Marian. 'I'll play over your shoulder if you don't mind. I didn't bring my rack.'

Marian felt every muscle tighten as though she were going to run a race, then she loosened every muscle. The Haydn Sonatas looked easy.

'Later we'll do the Beethoven Sonatas. They'll make you sit up,' said Alec. 'Ready?'

Marian laid her hands on the keys.

'Ah!' sighed the first stroke of Alec's bow.

Marian's mind, and her mind only, asked a question — 'Is there light enough?' Yes, there was light enough. She turned the page — thank Heaven! there was to be no polite foolishness about turning pages!

The delicate music filled the room, penetrated to other rooms, passed out through the open windows to the side street, drifted faintly across to where Lee sat with Nellie Roper.

'What's that?' asked Nellie sharply.

'Alexander LeConte, that red-haired boy who played in church, is over there playing with Marry.' Lee answered indifferently, her eyes straining into the darkness.

'Let's go over and sit on your terrace,' proposed Nellie. 'Thrilling!'

'I'd rather not,' objected Lee. To have Nellie there when Lucien arrived — never! 'Marry doesn't like an audience. We can hear well enough where we are.' She knew that Nellie looked at her curiously, but she did not care. She cared but for one thing.

'They say he's perfectly marvelous,' said Nellie. 'They say he's a genius. Don't you adore him?'

'Adore him!' mocked Lee. 'I think he's a nuisance.'

'Oh, listen!' cried Nellie. 'You sit here if you want to. I'm going over and walk up and down.'

There were other persons walking up and down — but no tall, straight Lucien. Hot tears welled in Lee's eyes.

'He'll come and go right in. I can't speak to him before all these — these' — Lee succumbed to a youthful impulse — 'these rubbernecks.' She left her chair and sat on the step, looking, looking, trying not to listen to the music which seemed to pierce like a dagger to her heart. She pressed her hand to her side. 'I'm so unhappy!'

In the sitting-room, Mamma played solitaire, on and on, on and on. The sunset faded, the moon rose. She did not look out. She touched a button and a soft light illuminated the room and her, especially her. She looked up frequently at her reflection in a gilt-framed mirror above the fireplace. The mirror was tipped forward, she could see all her plump, pale blue figure.

A red tide swept her face. Why did not Lucien come? The years were passing, the years were passing. Marian was busy with the doors closed, Lee was away — there was not often so free a field. She thought once more of laying her head on his shoulder. Old sensations returned, quickening to pain. She rose and stood near the front window — if Marian and her red-haired boy would stop only for a moment their incessant clamor!

At ten o'clock came Lee, sullen and angry.

'It's like the calliope at a circus. There are forty
people walking up and down. If she doesn't stop
soon, I wish you'd make her stop. I'm going to
bed.'

'Forty people walking up and down!'

'Or leaning against our fence!'

Mamma went to the door. She did not see Lucien,
but many admiring persons saw her from the distance. Their observation was consoling.

Marian and Alec played through a Haydn Sonata,
then another, then another. Neither paid the other
any compliments, each took excellence for granted.
Sometimes Alec looked round the room, at the old
portraits and the candlesticks and the vases and the
rare furniture. He knew little about periods, or the
superiority of one style of furniture over another,
but this room, he could tell, was very fine. He
closed the volume of Haydn and placed before
Marian the Mendelssohn Concerto.

'I'm to play the first movement for Bergmann.'

'That!'

'That.'

'For Bergmann!'

'Yes, in Philadelphia, in August.'

'Isn't that — rash?'

'Rather.'

'I don't know much about violin music, but I
know what that is. Everybody great plays it.'

'And all the fools,' said Alec grimly.

'Let's get to work! Perhaps we're not fools.'

Marian's gleaming eyes traveled down the page, she turned to the next. 'What you'd better do is to practice it every day.'

'You mean you'll practice with me?'

'I will.'

'Ready!'

'*Allegro, molto appassionato!*' read Marian. 'At sight! what do you take me for? Ready!'

'Crescendo!' ordered Alec. 'Now a great crescendo!'

'Whew!' whistled Marian under her breath.

'Soft!' ordered Alec. 'Now louder! Let's do that again from D. Tranquil as moonlight, but keep her up to time. Good! Lightly! Louder with your left hand! Now listen to me murder the cadenza!'

The cadenza was not murdered. Clear and clean, it filled the room, the house, the night. It died away; the piano, catching the notes as though they were spent balls, supported them.

'Back to the first theme!' ordered Alec. 'Now the second, tranquilly! Now the close. Faster! Faster!'

Alec laid down his bow. His color came and went, the birthmark was now pale, now bright. 'Some piece!' said he. 'You should have sent me packing long ago!'

Marian laughed. She had forgotten that Lucien was at hand, he would be sitting across the hall with Mamma. Excited by the music, she felt that she must see him instantly. Lucien loved music, he said that he did. He was not unbecomingly ardent as she

was; his nature was deep and strong rather than ex-
citable, and his temper was always judicial.

Mamma was sitting with her cards before her and
there was no Lucien in sight. She spoke in her
sweetest tone, as though to a small child — 'Bedtime, darling!'

Marian was determined that Mamma should not
be rude. 'Didn't you like our playing?'

'You mean practicing, darling.'

There was no doing anything with Mamma in this
mood of perversity. But she herself could be especially polite to Alec.

'Where's Lee?'

'In bed this long time.' Mamma was gathering
her cards and lowering the windows and raking the
ashes together, her air martyr-like.

Marian walked across the terrace with Alec, and
down the brick walk clear to the gate. Alec spoke
about the house. She stood with her hands on the
gate, while his eyes roamed above her, to each side
of her, his gaze sweeping the trees, the white pillars,
the antique urns.

'Marvelous,' said he. 'Good-bye, till to-morrow
morning!'

Marian continued to stand at the gateway. The
moon was high in the heavens and the beauty of the
night made her feel faint. A tall figure emerged from
the shadows and approached her directly. If only
one's heart were larger so that it could feel joy without feeling pain!

'Lucien!'

Lucien reached the gate. The moon slipped behind the summit of a tall oak, the two human figures
were in shadow.

'Where have you been?'

'I heard the music and I walked up and down the
side street.' Lucien spoke calmly, painful raptures
were not for him.

'All evening!' Then Lucien did indeed like
music!

'A good part of the evening.'

'It was Alexander LeConte and I.'

'I could see you through the windows.'

His hand slid along the rail and rested on hers. If
she had had a single experience of love-making she
would have turned her hand palm upward. But she
had had no experience and she let it remain as it was,
a hard, clenched lump. Lucien looked at her with
longing which was not physical desire, but a sort of
homesickness. The unresponsiveness of the slender
hand recalled his old humiliation. 'He bores me
to death, simply to death!' Marian was so danger-
ously bright, so alarmingly accomplished. This boy
was said to have genius and to play brilliantly, but
he did not play too well for her to play with him.
And Mamma was too old, and there was no one else
of whom Lucien ever thought.

'Alexander's to play for Bergmann.' Lucien's
hand was gone, but she felt no acute disappointment,
this was enough to dream of. She went on in a

shaken voice. 'I'm going to play his pieces over and
over with him. Won't you come in?'

'It's too late.' Lucien was deeply depressed —
this was his fate, always to be turned away when he
wished to linger. It was this time his sense of pro-
priety which turned him away.

'Bedtime, darling!' called a voice from the terrace.
It was a lovely voice, but in it was a note of irritation.

'Hark!' laughed Marian. 'Good-night!'

She sped fleet-footedly up the brick walk,
through patches of light and shadow, under the
pillars into the lighted doorway. Mamma was vanishing offended, up the stairs.

'I should guess that your musical friend lacks
breeding,' she said acidly over her shoulder.

Marian made no answer. She went about to see
whether Mamma had locked the windows and
thoroughly extinguished the fire. She had done
neither. What would Mamma say if she knew that
it was Lucien who kept her at the gate? Mamma
thought Lucien was her property. She laid the back
of her hand to her burning cheek. Upstairs a door
closed with decision. The house was perfectly still.
She went back into the sitting-room and held Lucien's picture in her arms and gazed upon the dap-
pled lawn. Moonlight, Mendelssohn, Lucien!

II

MAMMA

I

MAMMA appeared at the breakfast-table at eight o'clock. All the windows were open, but the shutters were bowed so that no sun should enter. As soon as Marian finished her breakfast she would close the shutters — this was the only way to be comfortable in the warm day advancing upon them. The flowers gathered yesterday afternoon were still fresh, the table was immaculate. Marian was at the table, beginning her substantial breakfast. She worked or taught or practiced till noon — there was every reason for a substantial breakfast.

'I thought if the house was to be filled with music' — Mamma believed that she was quoting accurately from some great poem — 'I might as well arise.'

Marian looked up brightly. Marian always began the day well, in composure and good spirits.

'The strains of that instrument rang in my ears all the livelong night,' continued Mamma sweetly.

Mamma did look a little seedy, but Marian made neither apologies nor promises. The proportion of the family income earned by her music was large, and here was a chance to improve her playing such as she might never have again. She felt in finger-tips

and elbows the urge of Alec's bow. Even after she
married Lucien, she would keep practicing hours
every day. Lucien was in her thoughts every moment, quickening her heartbeats, sending the blood
into her cheeks. Her affection had the possessive-
ness of maternity and all its desire to labor for the
beloved object. She wished to take care of Lucien,
to mother him, to see to his clothes, his meals.

'I shall probably have to arrange to leave the
house in the mornings if you are to keep it up,' went
on Mamma.

'It's to last for two weeks only,' explained Marian
pleasantly. 'Then Alec has a musical engagement in
Baltimore, and afterward he's to play for Bergmann.'

If Marian expected Mamma to be impressed, she
was disappointed. Mamma had reached her chair
and she sat down heavily. What had disturbed her
in the night was not music, she had no memory for
musical strains; it was the harassing and terrible
recollection that this was the first of the month.
What had brought her down an hour earlier than her
usual hour was the expectation of finding beside her
plate a long blue envelope, containing a long thin
slip of blue paper, signed by Judge Thrasher and
providing her with one hundred dollars for her own
use.

Marian would also have an envelope, but hers
would contain two hundred dollars, which was man-
ifestly and grossly unfair, even though she did pay
Celeste and the grocer and the plumber and the tax-

collector. In the first place, it was unsuitable that a daughter should receive more than a mother; in the second place, Marian did not need so much since she was able to make her own dresses and look well in them. Lee also would have a check, but that would be only fifty dollars until she was twenty-one.

Marian's mail was gone from beside her plate, but Mamma's and Lee's were still in place. The blue envelope lay uppermost — Mamma lifted it with her plump and jeweled hand. Below were other envelopes of white commercial paper, with commercial cards in the corners — 'The Dress Shoppe,' 'The Hat Shoppe,' 'Louise, Robes et Manteaux.' On all days of the month but this, these words brought most pleasant thoughts to Mamma's mind, of rich fabrics, of sweet scents, of high-heeled French slippers, of sweet-voiced clerks who called her 'My dear!' and who paid enchanting compliments to her and to Lee, the partner in her shopping excursions. 'Oh, the darling thing!' they would say. 'But you can't be old enough to be her mother!' Lee with her blond curly hair and her slightly upturned nose and her black eyes was a darling thing.

It was to Mamma directly that they paid the frankest of their compliments, as though they could not help themselves. 'Stout! If I had your eyes and your hair and your complexion, I should worry about being stout!' Excited, they slightly trilled their r's. 'Madame, the whole secret is to keep your complexion and your hair, let nothing else worry you. Figures aren't as important as they were five years ago.'

At Louise's shop, most elegant and expensive of all, the clerks called Louise herself to see how well Mamma looked in light blue, in dark blue, in pale rose, in white. Louise, a short heavy woman in a very short dress, said little; she simply spread her hands in a gesture of admiration. The gesture became by the least twist one of amazement if Mamma demurred or protested that she was not a millionaire. The letter from Louise's shop referred to her white dress with its heavy embroidery of grapes and leaves.

Mamma had a desperate hope, as foolish as it was desperate. 'What are you going to do with all your money, Marian, dear?'

'It's gone,' answered Marian shortly. 'Butcher's bills, plumber's bills, food — checks made out and in the letter box.'

'The Bon Air merchants would have waited, darling! Your promptness is absurd.'

'I still have Celeste's wages to earn before the end of the month, Mother' — this title only about twice a year. 'Unless you can help me?'

'Of course you wouldn't think of selling an old chair or a footstool or something?'

'We've talked that over finally.' Marian's tone was serene.

'We might starve first, I suppose.'

'We shan't starve.'

Lee drifted in to her light breakfast. All Lee's meals were light; more and more alarmed by her mother's figure, she limited herself to the least amount of food upon which life could be sustained. She ate no bread or potatoes, touched no butter, and ate only a little meat.

'There's your check, Lee.'

'I see.' Lee's voice was high-pitched but clear and sweet.

'You don't look very well,' commented Mamma.

'I didn't sleep,' complained Lee. 'I thought yesterday was a horrid day, with that screaming woman in church, and that Jew looking us over, and the burned dinner, and the screeching fiddle in the evening.' Lee knew that her allusion to elegant Mr. Obenchain hurt Mamma, she hoped that her allusion to Alec hurt Marian.

But Marian was not hurt. 'I have nothing against the Jews,' said she. 'Some of the most learned and most highly cultivated men in the world have been Jews.' She rang the bell for Celeste.

Celeste entered attired properly in a black dress, white apron and cap. At her worst she was insufferable, at her best she was superb. She had now the demeanor of the justly chastised penitent.

'I has to 'pologize fo' mah yestaday's behavioh,' she said. 'I sees de wrong I done. I 'pologizes to you, Miss Mabel, fo' de burnin' ob de chicken an' de beans and whatevah else was burned besides. I 'pologizes to you also, Miss Lee. I 'pologizes mos'

ob all to you, Miss Mahian, fo' de burned commod-
ities and fo' de extra labo's in which I involves you
on de Lo'd's day. I supprise de Lo'd accep' me in de
baptizin'. I supprise He didn't leave me drown. If
dese gem'men what was out front sees me in mah
red cap an' mah tantrums, I 'pologizes to dem. I
cheerfully cooks a comp'ny dinnah to make up
fo' —— '

'That's all right, Celeste,' interrupted Marian.
'We accept your apologies. You bring some fresh
toast for Miss Lee.'

Mamma ate slowly, as though her food were un-
savory and to be swallowed only by a great effort.
That upon which she chewed was really not toast
and canteloupe, it was words like 'Dress Shoppe'
and 'Hat Shoppe,' and abbreviations like 'dr.' and
'cr.'

'It's ridiculous to spell "shop" with two *p*'s and
an *e*,' she declared irritably. 'It makes one think of
"shoppy."'

'Isn't Celeste a scream?' said Marian pleasantly.

Mamma tried to fix her thoughts upon Celeste,
but failed. She lifted the envelopes; there was one
at the bottom which had escaped her notice until
this moment. 'Obenchain and Borleis' said the
printing in the corner. Obenchain and Borleis —
Mamma's mind wandered — Celeste — a dinner —
magnificent dinners probably given by Mr. Obenchain and Mr. Borleis — Lucien — a luncheon — a
dinner — what might not Mr. Obenchain do in re-

turn? Her thoughts arrived at last at their accustomed goal. She saw herself in white lace, in cloth of
gold, in silver, in pale blue, in black — but not yet,
though she was most magnificent of all in black.
Evening dress — a dinner, never a luncheon! She
saw her beautiful arms and neck in candle-light, she
saw — she saw, alas! her many envelopes.

'What are you going to do with your riches, Lee?'
she inquired, to flee her own thoughts.

'I'm going to have my check cashed, then I'm going to town to spend it,' answered Lee in her bright
little voice.

'I'll go with you,' said Mamma. She could look
at dresses while Lee bought. She would forget these
hateful envelopes. They had by this time the appearance of insolence, letters containing gross duel-
compelling abuse could have been no worse. Perhaps during the day something would happen. That
was always Mamma's hope.

II

Mamma and Lee walked up the street, Lee ac-
commodating herself unwillingly and unevenly to her
mother's slow gait. Mamma wore a dark blue dress
and hat, and a string of pearl beads. Her stockings
were dark blue; the wearing of dark stockings rather
than light was her only acknowledgment of forty-
five years. Even her suède shoes were dark blue.
They were tiny shoes on very beautiful feet. Lee
wore a white shirtwaist and a white pleated skirt, a

blue silk coat without sleeves, and a close-fitting blue hat. Both costumes were fashionable, elegant, and becoming. Lee's dress was not made by Marian; she did not wear Marian's creations when she went abroad.

The street was wide, and across it met the boughs of tall elms. Here and there stood an oak, the remnant of a forest. All the Bon Airians were gardeners, and before the houses, and in beds beside the houses, and in borders which separated one property from another were peonies and delphiniums and pansies and early roses. There were also many flowering shrubs, and towering above them several varieties of magnolia for which this was the most northern habitat. At this hour in the morning Bon Air seemed like Paradise, and a deserted Paradise. Housewives were at their tasks, clerks had taken their places behind counters, and lawyers were at their desks.

Where the two main streets crossed, one running exactly east and west, the other exactly north and south, there was a large open square, and in the center the Colonial Court House. Round the Square stood a few stately houses with wide yards, a row of stores, and a row of low buildings in which Lucien and other lawyers had their offices and to which some wicked wit had given the name Rogues' Row. In the street before the Court House waited a commodious and ancient omnibus, discarded by some city transportation company, and, besides two passenger trains a day, Bon Air's only certain connection with the world.

Mamma was happy, and, being happy, she talked pleasantly, smoothly, incessantly. Shutting the drawer upon her batch of envelopes she put all worries aside. She was even enough of a child to think of fairies coming and carrying the hateful bills away.

'If Nellie Roper should marry Allen Thrasher she would surely wish you to be one of her bridesmaids, if not her maid-of-honor,' said she to Lee.

'I don't believe she's engaged yet.'

'Oh, yes, she is! I know the signs, darling!' Mamma spoke with a gay superiority. 'You must insist upon a becoming color. I've seen weddings ruined by unbecoming colors. I declared at Olive Thrasher's wedding that I would never go to another rainbow wedding while I lived. The colors made even the guests look homely. I suppose' — they had reached the Square and Mamma glanced right and left, not with the tremulous fears of age, but with the shrinking of delicate femininity — 'I suppose Lucien's in court. I heard the bell ring.'

Lee looked at the Court House, at Rogues' Row, up the street, down. She looked everywhere, her eyes burning, but there was no sign of Lucien.

'I'm going to the Bank to get this check cashed.' She ran across the street. It would not be at all strange if Lucien were in the Bank. But Lucien was not, and she returned to Mamma.

Flushing with exertion Mamma climbed into the bus. She thought bitterly of the old furniture, and longingly of a new automobile, and resentfully of Marian. They chose seats unwittingly over the wheel where the motion was most violent and riding most rough. The seats were slippery and their black covers looked as though they might rub off.

'I'd turn up my skirt if I were you,' advised Mamma with a sigh.

The chauffeur came from the cigar store, complaining because there were no other passengers. 'When you folks gets an automobile, it won't be worth while runnin' the bus. Think o' gettin' one?'

'Sometime,' answered Mamma, though that happy day was remote. 'You'll have to pay my fare, I'm afraid, Lee, darling.'

The chauffeur collected the fares, climbed to his seat and started the engine, thus putting an end to all conversation. The road was unimproved, and the motion of the car was not only forward, but from side to side. Mamma sat with hands folded and eyes closed; after especially violent bumps she uttered a little shriek and looked about as though to be certain that she was still upon earth.

Lee sat with wide-open eyes. At the end of the town, they passed Lucien's house which was almost as beautiful as their own, where he lived with deaf Johnson and deafer Millie. Perhaps he had not yet gone to court, perhaps he might be seen walking thither. But there was no Lucien.

The bus rumbled on. The few villages through which they passed were not interesting, the heat grew increasingly oppressive. Beads of perspiration covered Mamma's pretty upper lip. At last after two hours they began to pass semi-detached houses, then solid city blocks. Hearing the bell of a trolley car, Mamma opened her eyes and mopped her brow.

'Ah!' she gasped, as though the Atlantic Ocean had been safely crossed. She opened her blue velvet bag and took from it a mirror and a powder puff. She applied powder to her face, then took a long look and smiled. Heat was uncomfortable, but not always unbecoming.

The bus came to a halt. 'Here's where you ladies gets off, ain't it?'

'Yes, Charles.'

'And you're goin' along back?'

'Yes, Charles.'

'Well, I ain't waitin' an hour for you, remember! The last time you traveled with me I got a notice to keep to the schedule. It was no polite notice, neither.'

'All right, Charles.'

Mamma stepped down, then Lee. Mamma's blood was coursing rapidly through her veins. The city was the place for life, for adventure; if she had been born in a city her experiences would have been more nearly those to which her beauty entitled her. She met the eyes of a strange gentleman; though he was much younger than she, he looked at

her and not at Lee. He looked not only admiring but
startled, even astounded. It was an effect which she
often produced. She took Lee's arm and together
they went slowly up the shady side of a steep
street.

'It's warm,' sighed Mamma. 'I'm glad we didn't
put this trip off.' She spoke as though the trip were
a long-planned and pressing necessity.

The shop of Louise was at the top of the hill, the
first in a section of little shops and large prices.
Having reached its vicinity, Mamma did not advance.

'Here's Louise's,' said Lee impatiently. 'Don't
you know where you are, Mamma?'

Mamma was pausing deliberately. She still held
to Lee's arm and with the other hand she pointed.

'Behold!' she cried, dramatically.

Lee followed her gaze and her pointing finger. In
enormous letters, black and white by day and flaming fire by night, stood the words, 'Obenchain and
Borleis.' Lee was about to say, 'It sounds like
Jerusalem!' but instead she looked at Mamma intently. The thought of Lucien and Mamma was
odious, against nature, but if Mamma wished to
make an alliance with some rich and great man —
that was different. Stepping back so that Mamma
might precede her into Louise's shop, she regarded
her with kindly criticism. There was no doubt that
she was very beautiful.

Mamma did not proceed, she stood still, and again

and in another direction she extended a pointing and dramatic finger.

'Lee!' she cried, faintly. 'Lee!'

In truth, Louise's projecting show-window framed an attractive picture. First of all, on the floor was a carpet of pale blue velvet, laid loosely down, and rising here and there in little waves tipped with light. Across a black Windsor chair lay a dress of silvery white brocade with shoulder straps of velvet ribbon the exact color of the velvet carpet. The foundation of the brocade was a fine net, so delicate that, though the material had the appearance of elegance, it could have little weight. At the waist was a blue water-lily of silk and across the skirt trailed a long necklace of crystals, dropped with apparent carelessness.

Both Mamma and Lee flushed; few women would have been unstirred by the sight. The dress was an object of beauty in itself, like a statue or a vase.

'In all the world there's nothing more —— ' Mamma hesitated. 'More transcendent,' she concluded in a solemn tone.

Passers-by saw them standing and joined them and they stepped out of the little crowd and went indoors. Within, four young ladies sitting on a bench rose as though propelled by a single spring. They were known to the trade as Marie, Pauline, Evangeline, and Lucie. Mamma and Lee knew them by their first names and they knew Mamma and Lee. They knew that Mamma paid slowly, but that ultimately she paid. They knew that Lee bought inexpensive dresses, but that she paid cash. They knew also that upon the two clothes looked better than upon any other customers, from Baltimore or outside Baltimore.

'Good-morning,' said Mamma brightly.

'Good-morning,' responded the four young ladies.

'We've been looking for you,' said one. 'I said yesterday that I had a dress for Mrs. Young and at least a dozen for Miss Lee.'

'Miss Lee's the buyer this morning,' explained Mamma. 'I'm merely the advisor.'

Behind Mamma's back the eyes of the young ladies met. Led by Lucie, Mamma and Lee stepped into a little room lined with mirrors, furnished with a table and two easy-chairs, a frame upon which to hang many dresses, and a platform upon which to stand while hems were adjusted. Lucie turned on an electric fan which stirred the air above their heads. She took Mamma's blue velvet bag and laid it on the table. Mamma sat back in an easy-chair sighing with happiness.

'Evening dresses?' said Lucie to Lee. 'Afternoon? Sports?'

Lee had taken off her blue coat. 'Sports.' She always knew what she wanted. 'Something of this kind but very cool. If you have two at no more than twenty-five dollars each, I'll take them.'

Mamma laughed. 'My frank child!'

'That's what we like,' said Lucie. She vanished and reappeared, laden with dresses. Marie followed close upon her heels with another armful, blues and pinks and yellows and greens. 'Any color goes this summer.'

'No yellow,' objected Lee. 'I hate it. And not that' — Lee picked up the dresses and laid them one by one aside. 'Or that, or that. There's one I'll try, and there's another.'

'Only those?'

'They'll be enough, if they're what I want. How much are they?'

'Bargains, my dear. The Madame feels she's a little overstocked. This is twenty, this twenty-five. Aren't you surprised? But only to our regular customers.'

Lee stood in a single garment of pale pink silk.

'Shocking the way they dress!' commented Mamma lightly. But Mamma was thinking regretfully of her youth with its quilted petticoats, its corset, its corset cover, its long sleeves and trailing skirts.

'Oh, no, it's not shocking,' laughed Lucie. 'It's cool and sensible and appropriate to youth.'

Outside were voices, now in the room to the right, now in the room to the left. The voice to the right was complaining.

'I got this dress home, and I couldn't think it was as becoming as I thought it was here.'

'Let's try it on again.' The voice of Evangeline

was as sweet as the voice of Mamma. 'Now
what's the trouble with it? I think it's most becoming.'

'It looks better than it did at home,' conceded the
voice, now no longer complaining but pleased. 'How
do you account for it?'

'What time of day did you try it on? In the morning, by natural light?'

'I believe it was.'

'And had you curled your hair?'

'No.'

'Madame, the Queen of Sheba would have looked
homely in this dress or in any other evening dress
under such circumstances. You try it again — this
evening. Now, was there anything else you wanted?
We have darling sports dresses at a special price.
Let me show them to you.'

'Well' — the voice was doubtful, as though there
might be envelopes in a desk drawer. It was also
apologetic, as though something were owing Louise
and her store in recompense for this uncertainty
about their wares. 'I might try a few.'

From the other side came a voice which was tense,
rapt, thrilled and thrilling. 'I'm going to be married,
and I've come to buy my trousseau.'

There was a chorus of congratulations; delicate
scents drifted in, other voices. Lee had put on a
dress made of a pleated skirt and a sleeveless scarlet
coat. She looked into the glass and blushed at her
own prettiness. Her upturned nose really made no

difference whatever. 'What do you think of this, Mamma?'

'Exactly right.' Mamma spoke with the sudden eagerness of one recalled from dreaming. Her mind was upon the waves of light blue velvet, upon the azure water-lily, upon blue velvet shoulder straps against pink flesh, upon a chain of heavy square-cut crystals, more magnificent than any diamonds, crystals emitting little opalescent gleams. She saw soft light falling from glittering chandeliers, smelled the smoke of strong, expensive cigars, saw a table spread with delicacies with French names.

Lee stepped out of the red-and-white dress, and into a pink dress.

'Adorable!' cried Lucie.

'That's sweet,' said Mamma. She determined to keep her mind upon the matter in hand. It was like struggling to keep one's head above boisterous waves.

'I'll take both,' said Lee briskly.

Oh, to be like Lee, to be able to wear home-made things a part of the time! Oh, to be like Lee in an-other way — to spend one's money after one had it, and not before! To be able to wear twenty-five-dollar things like Lee!

Lucie gathered up the dresses, those Lee had selected and the others, and carried them all out. She returned so quickly that she must have dropped them, or some one must have taken them from her

arms. In her hands, carried like the Queen's robe,
was the dress of brocade.

'Mrs. Young ——'

Mamma lifted her hands, terror in her eyes. 'No!'
she shrieked lightly. 'No!'

'I don't ask that you buy it.' Lucie's calm voice
had in it the inflection with which one soothes
hysteria. 'Indeed, you couldn't wear it, it's two
sizes too small. I ask you only to slip it over your
head. It's without exception the most beautiful
gown we've ever had in the shop. I think it's the
most beautiful I've ever handled in my life. The
difficulty is that it's both youthful and adult. It
should be worn by a woman, and not by a girl, but it
must be a woman who's an absolutely faultless
blonde, with plenty of color.'

As in a dream, Mamma removed her dress. She
closed her eyes, the hand of Lucie smoothed powder,
sprinkled on her neck. The brocade dress had the
softest silk lining; it passed down over her neck and
arms. She kept her eyes closed. Last of all came the
crystals, cool as a snake. She opened her eyes, and
at once began to tremble. She saw in the mirror herself and smiling Lucie and staring Lee. Lee looked
at her as the amazed strangers looked. She had received many compliments, but none equal to the expression in Lee's eyes. She saw in another second
Louise. Whatever might be the racial origin of Lucie
and Marie and Evangeline and Pauline, there was
no doubt about that of Louise. Her thick iron-gray

hair curled in tight waves, her black eyes gazed
piercingly at Mamma. She gazed first at Mamma,
then at Lucie.

'You said it was too small. It's not in the least
degree too small. It's exactly right.'

'I was mistaken,' confessed Lucie. 'I was never
more surprised.'

Louise came forward so that she might inspect
Mamma directly and not merely her reflected image.
Her cheek flushed. The dress was wonderful, but
Mamma in it was far more wonderful.

'Madame, if I looked as you do in that dress, I
would beg, I would pawn, I would steal rather than
not have it.'

She spoke as one who contemplates an act of
monstrous sacrifice; then she departed instantly, as
though she would not endure seeing the sacrifice
consummated.

Mamma closed her eyes. 'Take it off of me instantly!' she begged in a faint tone.

'I haven't offended you, have I?' asked Lucie. 'I
had no idea it would fit you. It was for my own
pleasure. Would you be willing to let the other girls
see it?'

'I couldn't object to that.'

Evangeline uttered a scream. 'If we could only
put you in our window!'

Pauline laughed. 'And wouldn't the buyer be
fooled unless she could get Mrs. Young to wear the
dress for her?'

'We haven't a great deal of time,' said Lee impatiently.

'It's far too young for me,' declared Mamma, feeling the silken surface slip off, not in alarm as she had felt it slip on, but with a deeper woe.

Lucie spoke with passion. 'It isn't one's age, it's what one looks well in.'

Mamma and Lee went down the street.

'I think I'll stop before lunch and have my hair cut,' planned Lee. 'Then I won't need to stir out of the hotel till the bus leaves.'

Mamma entered the Beauty Shoppe with Lee and stood waiting until she learned that Lee could be attended to at once.

'Facial, Madame?' said the clerk to Mamma.

'No'— there was one economy Mamma could accomplish, she needed as yet no facials.

'Hair cut, Madame?'

Mamma trembled on the brink. She had a hundred times trembled on the brink. For the hundred and first time a youthful hand pushed her out of peril.

'No!' Lee answered the clerk savagely. 'No! Of course not! Mamma, you wait for me at the Bellevue.'

Mamma walked to the corner, her step growing slower and slower. She met for once no eyes of admiration, though many such eyes gazed upon her. She walked round the block. She walked round the block again, though noontide heat poured down and once more perspiration beaded her lip. She returned to the window of the shop of Louise. It was not Louise's custom to tag with their prices the exhibits in her window, but, in returning the white dress to its place, Lucie had left the ticket exposed. The price was three hundred dollars. Mamma gave a start; then she said defiantly aloud, 'Not a penny too much!' She walked away. Within, on their bench, breathless, watching Mamma with eagle eyes, sat Evangeline and Pauline and Lucie and Marie.

'Lucie!' shrieked Marie. 'Stop it! You're hugging me to death!'

III

Tossed from side to side in the bus, Mamma and Lee rode homeward. There were two other passengers, residents of Bon Air whom Mamma knew by sight only, and they prevented her talking and gave Lee an excuse for silence. From a hilltop Mamma looked back. High above the city she saw in great letters 'Obenchain and Borleis,' and the recollection of Louise's shop and the white brocade dress became a keen pain.

'Life will soon be past,' she sighed, though she was only a little over forty-five. 'It's a pity that I can't have one really handsome dress. I never had a dress that cost three hundred dollars. It's possible to pay a thousand for a dress.' She found to her confusion that she was speaking aloud. Happily the noise of the engine drowned her voice.

Lee sat with her elbow on the window-sill, looking first at the city streets, then at the pleasant fields, and seeing nothing. She was once more as unhappy as she could be. She had been absent from home all day and it was as though Lucien had been possessed by Marian. She had begun to think of Mamma as negligible; if Lucien had wanted Mamma he would have taken her long ago. He was learned and intelligent; he would not choose a wife who knew as little as Mamma. Marian was different; he talked with her about hateful books, and glances sometimes passed between them which betokened a private understanding.

In the end, as twilight descended upon the fields, her spirits brightened. Beside her on the seat lay the box containing her new dresses, to which she had added a white felt hat. She had been away all day, but now she was going back. Marian's morning would have been given to playing, her afternoon to labor, and it was very unlikely that she had even seen Lucien. They passed Lucien's fields, his house. There was a light in the dining-room where he was clearly having his dinner. At least he was not with Marian now.

When the bus stopped in the Square and the other passengers alighted, Mamma leaned forward and spoke to the chauffeur. 'I wonder whether you wouldn't drive us to our door,' she pleaded sweetly. 'We're very, very tired.'

'I guess I can.' Charles did not speak sweetly.

He frequently performed this extra service for Mrs. Young and also for other persons, but the other persons gave him an extra quarter of a dollar and she did not.

Their own street was fairly smooth. In the light from the car, they could see the massive trunks of the trees and the green foliage. Bon Air had, after all, its charm.

'Your hand, Lee,' said Mamma when the car stopped before the brick gateway. In public she liked to appear agile and brisk, but she was now where négligé behavior was permissible and where négligé attire would soon be assumed.

Marian stood at the door, opening it for them. 'Welcome home! Tired?' Marian certainly gave no sign of being tired. She had doubtless had an easy day; they had had a very hard day. 'Supper's ready. I thought you'd be hungry.'

Poor and old as Mamma believed her home to be, she was glad to step within its doors. She saw herself poor and old also, matching it. The vague resignation of the aged for the first time filled her breast. If she were to be saved from the advance of age, it must be done quickly.

'We'll wash our hands and faces,' said she with a sigh. 'Then we'll be with you.'

'Tired?' Marian asked Lee again.

At sight of Marian, composed, cheerful, in her smooth white dress, Lee let the jealous wave overwhelm her better resolutions.

'No,' she said crossly, starting up the steps, her boxes in her hand.

Together in a few minutes, the three sat down. Marian looked round the room — what a beautiful, beautiful room it was with its carved mantelpiece, its gleaming furniture and shining silver! Mamma looked at the supper dishes set before her, which she was to serve. There were creamed sweetbreads and new peas; there were also hot biscuits, and there was currant jelly in its first unfaded glory of color.

'You didn't make currant jelly, Marian!'

'I made currant jelly,' said Marian. 'I had picked all the currants before you were up. After breakfast Celeste stemmed them while I practiced with Alexander LeConte. Then I made the jelly — fifty glasses. I took two to Mrs. Thrasher, and two to Mrs. Roper, and three out to Lucien's house. Then I came home and practiced, and here I am.'

Mamma was for an instant paralyzed by this catalogue. She felt an unreasonable anger — Marian had no business to be so capable, and her words were a reproach.

'And what did they all say?'

'They were all grateful and enthusiastic, naturally. I said you sent the jelly, Mamma. Lucien, of course, I didn't see; I gave the glasses to Millie.'

The flush on Lee's cheeks faded. 'You needn't give me so much food!' she said sharply. 'You know it takes away my appetite.'

Mamma kept the plate she had absently prepared

for Lee and passed her another on which there was a
teaspoonful from each dish. She would try to eat and
forget the brocade dress and the dreadful envelopes.
The contents of the envelopes were not all new; some
of the bills went back several months, and at the
foot was written, 'Please remit!' Last month a
dreadful man had come from Gates and Rath, where
she had bought her last winter's coat. He arrived
when she had callers in the drawing-room and made
a loud commotion on the porch. Marian persuaded
him to go away, and gave him from her own purse a
small sum on account; she must not forget to be
grateful to Marian for that.

Marian went on talking about her practicing.
Alec played gloriously; she was certain that he would
be famous, and they would be proud to know him.
The practicing was doing her the greatest good; she
wished that she could practice all day. She looked
from one face to the other, once again hopeful of a response. But she heard only a vague 'Yes, dear,'
from Mamma and no response whatever from Lee.
Mamma ate slowly; the delicious supper was like the
delicious breakfast, tasteless, but she ate a good deal
so as to occupy her mind. She remembered that they
had not bought even a handkerchief for Celeste.

'And you found a dress?' Marian asked Lee.

'She found two,' answered Mamma. 'Darling
dresses, for next to nothing. And poor Mamma got
none.' Her voice choked; again the recollection of
the white brocade overwhelmed her.

'But you have a surprise here!' Marian rose from the table and went into the hall. Returning, she carried a wooden box, addressed to Mrs. Osborne Young. 'It came by express from Baltimore.'

'Prepaid?' asked Mamma.

'Prepaid.'

'What can it be?' Mamma meant, really, 'From whom does it come?' She prayed that the donor might be he whom she imagined.

While they had their dessert, Celeste opened the wooden box and brought to light a white cardboard box. She set it down before Mamma.

'It's heavy, Miss Mabel! Weighs 'bout five pounds!'

'That's probably exactly what it weighs.' Mamma's excited laugh was, to speak accurately, a giggle. She lifted the lid. Within the cardboard box was a carved and inlaid box, within the carved and inlaid box was a beautifully decorated tin box. On the tin box lay a card — her fingers shook as she took it from its envelope. It was that which she desired with all her soul. 'With remembrances of a pleasant meeting, Mr. Henry Obenchain,' read she in a trembling voice.

'You've made a conquest.' Marian was pleased with her pleasure.

'Chocolate!' exclaimed Mamma! 'Eat, everybody! Marian! Lee!'

'Delectable!' cried Marian.

'You know I never eat candy.' Lee's voice was

strained and cold; she longed for candy with a mighty longing.

'Celeste! Celeste, bring a saucer and we'll give you a supply all for yourself.' Mamma need no longer be concerned about having forgotten Celeste's little gift.

She carried her present into the sitting-room. It was very expensive and beautiful; the inlaid box was intended to serve as an ornament or as a jewel box.

'It shall stand there.' She pointed to the table inside the sitting-room door. 'Where every one can enjoy it. I should think' — she had not yet entire control of her voice — 'I should think that's about as expensive a present as a gentleman should give a lady whom he doesn't know very well.'

'Whom he has seen only once,' said Marian with indulgence.

'And that only for five minutes,' added Mamma.

Marian returned to her piano. She wished that she had some way of sending word to Alec to come and play. But the LeContes had no telephone. Her mother was in the best of humors, it would be well to take advantage of it and practice till bedtime. Melodies rang in her ears, incomplete and fleeting, and an overpowering hunger filled her heart. She began to play Bach, and laid the music aside and played Beethoven from memory. In certain moods, when she was deeply stirred, she could play on and on, recalling compositions which she had never deliberately memorized.

Reaching the end of a sonata, she lifted her hands and looked at them, and laughed. She could not fancy them ever growing tired. She thought of Alec — he was like a burning flame. She smiled indulgently as she remembered his eagerness to play, and his absent-mindedness. He had come this morning without a necktie — perhaps that was what his mother had meant by the penalties of his acquaintance. Discovering his plight he blushed and laughed — 'Won't she have one on me!'

Lee went upstairs without a good-night. She would try on her dresses, then she would go wearily to bed.

Mamma sat at her desk, now looking at her inlaid box, now eating a piece of candy from the decorated tin box. She loved pistachio above all flavors and she picked out the pieces of chocolate with green ends. There had been twelve in the beginning and there were none now. Since Marian did not care for pistachio, and Celeste believed it poisonous, and Lee took none, she had eaten them all.

Biting the end of her penholder, she gazed at the note-paper spread before her; then rose and walked toward the hall. Once she crossed the hall and stood outside the drawing-room door; then, shaking her head as though she had intended to consult her daughter but decided not to do so, she returned to her desk. She held her head very high upon the return journey, apparently resolved upon some independent course of action.

She sat down, and, the music being loud, she put her thoughts into audible words so as to make them very clear. 'Luncheon?' A luncheon was soon over, and the bright light of midday was unpoetic and unsympathetic and unbecoming. Besides, no merchant prince could leave his business at noon! 'Dinner?' She shook her head. 'We couldn't be grand enough.' 'A country supper? Ah!' said Mamma. At a country supper, one need not be formal, but one could wear evening dress. She flushed a brilliant crimson, as though a light from a red-shaded lamp had suddenly been thrown upon her face. But it was the light from a white brocaded dress. Tears appeared in the corners of her beautiful eyes.

After a long while, she walked across the hall, and to Marian's side. Marian ceased playing at once and looked up.

'I'm thinking of giving a party.'

'Yes?' Marian's face blanched. She heard the sound of chattering voices — 'What's trump?' 'You renigged! I heard that he' — they had no money for parties, and she had no time; not until Alec was gone and the chance for playing with him over would she hear of a party. She folded her hands in her lap, by the tightness of her grasp admonishing herself to respect and at the same time to firmness.

'A supper party,' went on Mamma. 'A very select party of six.'

'What six?'

'You and Lee and I for the ladies, and Lucien and

Mr. Obenchain and your musical friend, if you wish
him, for the gentlemen. Say three weeks from this
evening.'

Marian's hands loosened. That would be Alec's
last evening. They would play for the company;
perhaps Mr. Obenchain would be able to do something for Alec by helping him to get an audience in
Baltimore. At any rate, it would be good for Alec to
play for Obenchain before he played for Bergmann.
Besides the first movement of the Mendelssohn
Sonata, he intended with equal daring to play
Wieniawski's Scherzo Tarentelle.

'I suppose your friend would have a dress suit,'
said Mamma.

'I suppose so,' answered Marian. 'Will it be as
formal as that?'

'Evening dress is not considered formal. The
gentlemen would surely pay us that compliment!'

Marian laid her hands on the keys. 'I'll see to the
supper,' she promised. 'It's a good thing that
Celeste has been baptized.'

Mamma laughed happily. That was what
Mamma was made for — happiness and the dispens-
ing of favors. She rose and went back to the sitting-
room and wrote a note and then copied it. It pleased
her immensely; it was grateful, but not too grateful. Mr. Obenchain must not think his favor the
only one she had ever received. Would Mr. Obenchain 'come to us informally'? The phrase she knew
was exactly right.

Then Mamma laid her hands on both sides of her desk. A struggle was taking place within her. She wrote another letter — 'Dear Madame,' it began. She tore it up, she wrote again. She sat motionless, rapt. Time passed, but she did not realize it. She sighed. She bent her head for a moment on her arms and sleep caught her. Marian came to the door.

'It's midnight, Mamma!'

She lifted her head. The second draught remained undestroyed, it was addressed to Louise. She carried it, together with the note to Obenchain, to the box outside the front door where the postman would get them when he brought the morning mail. He would surely come in the morning, because the hateful envelopes were always spread over two days at least.

Riding on a wave of hope, she ceased to remember the hateful envelopes. She had a little tune remembered from her youth which she sang when she was very happy and excited, and this she hummed while she undressed. Occasionally she pronounced a word or two — 'to me, Sweet Marie, to me, Sweet Marie,' and once a whole quatrain.

> 'Every daisy in the dell
> Knows my secret, knows it well,
> Yet to thee I dare not tell,
> Sweet Marie.'

IV

Mamma sat at the head of the table. It was the evening of the twenty-second of June and as intensely warm as Maryland can be, but she did not feel the heat.

She wore a white brocade dress with pale blue shoulder straps, an azure water-lily at her waist, and a long chain of crystals round her neck. The crystals were now soft, now bright, reflecting first the colors of her shoulder straps and cheeks and flesh, then the candle-light. Her cheeks were flushed with happiness, her beautiful face was uplifted, her smooth and plump neck and arms lay bare to the eyes of all. She was, to use Marian's expression, luscious; Marian could not keep her eyes away from her. Lee stared at her also, with a frightened look, as though competing with her were vain.

In Mamma's eyes was a happy consciousness of all the delights surrounding her; the house which this evening seemed to her beautiful, her handsome daughters, handsome Lucien, Obenchain's car outside her door to be admired of all.

To her right sat Obenchain, bearded, smooth-voiced, magnificent, evidently also very happy. Lee expressed repulsion for men with beards, but Mamma laughed, she had grown up in another generation. Half the men, she said, would look better with beards; as they were, they were effeminate. She cited Bon Air chins which fell away and mouths which were weak. She was more observant than you might expect. Obenchain, it was certain, would not care in the least what Lee thought. His eyes and mind and thoughts were for Mamma. His left arm, which was either undeveloped or slightly withered, was of little use, but he was not in the least awkward.

To Mamma's left sat Alec, his costume correct, his manners irreproachable. He was really passable in looks and very well-behaved, and Mamma was relieved. To her he had become an increasing annoyance. He arrived in the mornings exactly on the stroke of nine. She heard little conversation except directions in a fierce rude tone. 'Faster! Speed it up!' He called Marian by her first name. Sometimes he called her 'Marry.' 'Speed it up, Marry!'

He sat now quietly looking about and listening, his eyes and red hair shining. If Mamma had known what he thought, not of her house or of her daughter, but of her, she would have been appeased forever. He tried to picture Mamma in her youth — she could not possibly have been any more wonderful than now. Very complimentary names came into his mind — 'Hebe' was one, and 'Aphrodite' another. He was still not quite satisfied, and, struggling for a second to remember another name, said 'Saskia!' almost aloud. Mamma had Saskia's gold and ivory; she had other beauties which Saskia lacked.

Looking at Obenchain Alec sought for the name of another portrait, but Obenchain's costume seemed to lack some essential detail. Ah, he had it! There was a Whistler painting of a tall man, with a lady's coat across his arm and a broad ribbon across his breast — that was Obenchain, and the ribbon was what he lacked.

Opposite each other sat Marian and Lee, the one in white, the other in pale blue. Mamma had prescribed their dresses, believing it suitable that they should carry out the colors of her own. Marian was intensely happy and excited — here was assembled an intelligent company. She looked forward eagerly to the hour after dinner when she and Alec would play. Lee was not in the least happy. She was appalled by Mamma's beauty; she was smitten to the heart by the glances which passed between Marian and Lucien, and by the freedom with which they talked and laughed. She could talk to Lucien when they were alone; then he was interested in her and delighted with her, then he laughed at her wit. In company she was silent, gauche, what Marian called 'pure dumb-bell.'

At the head of the table sat Lucien, dignity incarnate, at once happy and sorrowful. This was his birthday, though no one knew it but himself — he was forty-one years old. Sometimes he felt a thousand, sometimes he felt youth returning in a wave. If he had long ago asked Mamma to marry him, he might be sitting at the head of the table as a right. Now, amazingly beautiful as she was, he desired Marian and not her. But he did a sum in subtraction and it terrified him — forty minus twenty-one equals nineteen; no, it was nineteen yesterday, now it was twenty. He heard again a high, clear voice, 'He bores me to death!' It was not unlike Marian's voice in moments of strong feeling. She used the same words often. 'Parties bore me to death!' 'Modern music bores me to death!' He determined that his agony should no longer continue; to-morrow — no, within the week — he would ask Marian to marry him.

The blue center-piece which Mamma requested was arranged in the silver bowl from which the Youngs had been baptized for generations. There was ageratum and butterfly bush and heliotrope, their blue relieved by sprays of valerian, baby's-breath, and maidenhair fern. The table was covered with old lace and set with old silver and old china and old glass. Obenchain looked smilingly from one object to another.

'You have most beautiful things!' said he.

Mamma was honest as the day except in the matter of paying bills promptly. 'They're all an inheritance of Marian's,' she explained. The allusion was fortunate; it gave her a chance to apologize to Obenchain for what must seem to him a very serious omission in the meal. 'Marian inherited something else from her,' she said, laughing. 'Confess, Marry.'

Marian laughed also, but in this matter she was adamant. 'She hated intoxicating liquor,' she explained sharply. 'We never have it, if that's what you mean, Mamma!'

'That's what I mean.' Mamma smiled at Obenchain.

For a while, as was suitable for the head of the family, Mamma kept the conversation under her control. She told, without visible connection with the subject of conversation immediately preceding, her story of Queen Victoria and Queen Eugénie. 'Victoria knew the chair was there, Eugénie had to look round to be sure. I tell my girls always to be Victorias. Don't I, Lee?' She was disturbed by Lee's sullen silence. This was a most inconvenient time for Lee to have a spell.

Lee answered only with an ungracious 'You certainly do, Mamma!' Under the table Lucien had accidentally touched Marian's foot or Marian had touched his, and they begged each other's pardon and laughed. Lee was more and more convinced that there was some secret understanding between them. She did no sums in subtraction; to her forty equaled twenty-one, or even eighteen.

Mamma had reached the end of her light entertainment, and she looked at Marian appealingly. Before the silence became uncomfortable, Marian asked Lucien what he had been reading, in a tone meant not for him alone but for everybody.

'Jefferson's letters, most recently.'

Mamma laughed. 'This is our high-brow friend,' said she to Obenchain. 'He brings up our average of intelligence.'

'Not so very high-brow,' insisted Lucien. 'Mr. Obenchain will know that.'

Obenchain turned toward Lucien. He had the

most polite way of giving the person with whom he
spoke the attention not only of his mind but of his
body.

'I've always been more interested in Jefferson
than in any other American. I possess a fairly good
collection of Jeffersoniana. I should like to show it
to you.'

'Oh, tell us what you have!' cried Mamma. This
was pretty good for Mamma, who did not really
know what Jeffersoniana were. Obenchain and
Lucien talked animatedly — they gave her temporarily entire relief from anxiety, and she could
gaze at the pretty table and eat slowly and smile.
She thought of her dress — it was the most beautiful
dress in the world; of Obenchain's car before the
door, of how beautifully Celeste was serving. She
had a green silk dress which she had promised
Celeste and which Marian had offered to cut down
for her. Marian was an angel, Celeste was an angel,
every one was angelic. Mamma felt like a bride
whom all serve and adore.

Lucien promised that he would visit Obenchain
and his collection. He knew, he said, of some Jeffersoniana which might be had.

'I fancy that the price which the owners would
consider very, very high, and which would quite set
them up for the remainder of their lives, would seem
very reasonable to you.'

'Mr. LeConte' — Mamma was ready with her
leading question — 'I suppose your reading is
limited entirely to music.'

'Oh, no!' said Alec. 'If you're going to play well, you have to know many things besides music.'

'And what have you been reading?'

'Oh, everything! I don't have any system. I can begin anywhere and learn things I don't know. I'm most interested in books on art, etchings in particular. I can never get enough of etchings. They're like violin music, wonderful things done with a few sharp strokes.'

Obenchain gave Alec the attention of his mind and body. 'That's a happy simile. You must see my etchings, both old and new, I have an early print of "Jo."'

'You have!'

'What is "Jo"?' asked Marian eagerly.

'It's a Whistler etching, the loveliest in the world,' explained Obenchain. He went on to tell of other etchings which he owned, not with boasting, but with pleasure in the prospect of showing them to his new friends. There was in his heart, as in Lucien's, a core of deep humility. Though he had been married twice, he believed that his crippled arm made him unattractive to women, and he was grateful to these kind people who had taken him in. As for Mamma, he had ceased to look at her for fear that his admiration might seem foolish. He saw her not only at her own table, but in greater, wider spaces than this room, himself at her side.

Only Lee, a dot outside the circle, would not be happy and interested and gay. Every one tried to

talk to her, even Alec whom she snubbed on all occasions, but she remained a dot outside a circle.
Mamma offered her many gentle openings, but she
would not be tempted to anything but monosyllabic
speech. Lucien looked at her distressed; she believed
that his distress was disapproval.

The young fowl were superbly roasted, the vegetables had been gathered only an hour before they were
cooked, the salad was Marian's best salad, the
mousse her most notable achievement. She had
been in the kitchen, apron-covered, brisk, expert,
until Obenchain's car glided to the curb.

It was not quite dark when they finished and they
went to the terrace to drink coffee. At rest, but fully
manned, waited Obenchain's car at the curb. Obenchain set down his cup — it was his third. He complimented not only the ladies and their possessions
but the food, all in the most delightful way.

'Would any one like to take a little ride? I visited
when I was here before a hill about a half-mile away
with a magnificent view. We can still get the sunset
glow.'

'It would be delightful!' Mamma longed to ride
in the beautiful car, and to have the citizens of Bon
Air see her riding in the beautiful car. 'It would cool
us off.' She was already on her feet.

'Alec and I will stay here and go over some music
to play for you when you come back,' said Marian.

'That will be fine,' answered Mamma instantly.
'Mr. Obenchain, this young man promises to be a

great virtuosa.' The word came to Mamma as un-
expectedly as a gift from Heaven. 'Lee, darling, get
Mamma her blue wrap.'

Lee ran indoors — Mamma and Mr. Obenchain,
she and Lucien — her eyes shone, her knees shook.

'I wonder if I mayn't stay and hear the practicing,' suggested Lucien, believing that Obenchain
would like to be alone with Mamma. Lee he forgot,
as though she did not exist. 'LeConte tells me he's
going away to-morrow and there's no telling when
we shall hear him again.' Lucien had still another
motive. This red-haired boy of no background
whom he had thought so wild-looking — Marian
could have no interest in him!

'As you like,' consented Mamma graciously.

Lee came with the pale blue wrap, and Obenchain
folded it about Mamma. He stepped back and she
walked down the brick path with Lee beside her.
He followed, revolving in his mind a pleasant plan.
He was an excellent judge of budding talent, and, if
this young man were promising, the arranging of his
future was simple. He helped Mamma into the car
and stood waiting for Lee. His hand enclosed
Mamma's lovely elbow, but Lee he dared not touch;
she was a young porcupine.

Lee paused, her foot on the step. 'Are none of the
others coming?' Lee's wail meant, 'Isn't Lucien
coming?'

'Didn't you hear what they said? Of course not!
you went for my wrap. Marian and her young

Paderewski' — Mamma said 'Paderuski' — 'prefer to play, and Lucien's going to listen to them. When we come back we're to have a lovely concert. Get in, darling.'

'I think I won't go,' said Lee steadily, withdrawing her foot. 'I remember that I promised to see Nellie Roper. 'I'll be right there on the porch,' she explained to Obenchain with a high-pitched laugh, pointing across the street. 'I can see you the minute you get back.'

'That will be all right,' agreed Mamma. 'Perfectly all right.'

Obenchain stepped in and sat down beside Mamma.

'Growing pains,' explained Mamma prettily. 'Immature and a little difficult. I suppose we were all like that.'

They drove slowly to the hill to find the view obscured by twilight. They drove a little farther and a little farther; naturally they did not overtake the sun. Their conversation was such as might safely have been heard by Obenchain's chauffeur and footman, though they did not talk about the sunset, but about themselves and each other. Their voices were wistful as well as low. The years were passing; many, many years were gone.

'So I had these two daughters to bring up,' sighed Mamma, as though her daughters had been four and one, instead of fourteen and eleven. 'It hasn't always been easy.'

'But you had them,' Obenchain reminded her. 'You weren't entirely alone.' He explained that he had been twice bereaved, both of his wives dying within a year after marriage.

'Ah!' mourned Mamma. 'That was hard.'

'It seems a long, long time ago,' sighed Obenchain. 'It is a long, long time ago.'

They drove still a little farther before they turned. Each knew by now all that did not appear on the surface of the other's life. Life, they agreed, was a very lonely business without the companionship of a contemporary.

'We must go back!' declared Mamma, feeling not so much the qualm of anxiety as a consciousness that she had no more to tell. 'What will my daughters think of me?'

'It's only ten-thirty,' said Obenchain. 'We aren't far from Bon Air I'm sure.'

Proper to the core, Mamma saw visions of accidents, of further delay. Mercifully there was no delay and the journey took but half an hour. There stood the house as they had left it, only less clearly outlined, and even lovelier.

'It's too late for me to come in except to say goodbye,' said Obenchain. The strains of the violin met them as they went up the path. 'Listen!' He laid his hand on Mamma's arm. The air was warm and aromatic with the breath of the woods. 'What a heavenly moment! The young man plays well.'

'Doesn't he!' Mamma spoke as though Alec belonged to her. 'I have great hopes of his future. I look forward to the time when we shall all be proud of him.'

Obenchain removed his hand and they walked on.

'A perfect gentleman,' said Mamma to herself.

They crossed the terrace and entered the hall. The drawing-room was a dark cave, except for the light on Marian's face and on the white page and on Alec's flaming hair. The music soared to a brilliant close.

'Surprisingly good intonation!' commented Obenchain.

'A lovely touch,' cooed Mamma. 'I've always thought his touch exquisite.' She walked to the door of the drawing-room followed by Obenchain's admiring and indulgent gaze. He regarded her as one might a beautiful child, to whom for whose beauty all was forgiven.

'Where's Lucien?' asked Mamma.

'Here.' Lucien replied from the darkest corner. He had satisfied himself that these two young people had nothing in common except youth and music. They talked to each other as gamboling pups might talk if they could speak.

'Where's Lee?'

'Isn't she with you?' cried Marian.

'Upstairs,' explained Lucien, advancing to the hall. 'I saw her pass the door long ago.' His calmness dispelled a foolish alarm in Marian's breast. Sometimes Lee's behavior angered her, sometimes it terrified her. Lee was deeply beloved, if exasperating.

'I must say good-night,' announced Obenchain. 'I trust this is the first of many pleasant meetings for us all. I've had a most happy evening. I shall write you and we shall make some plans. Mr. LeConte, I hope you'll believe me when I say that you play extraordinarily well. You get excellent tone, warm, even, full, vibrant. I've heard all the famous violinists and I believe that with maturing talent and hard work you can equal almost any of them.'

Alec grew pale, the birthmark glowed. 'I'd like awfully to believe you!'

'Mr. Clement, if you're going home, let me take you. Mr. LeConte?'

'We've got to play one thing over again,' answered Marian for Alec. 'We bungled it. I hope you'll both come back soon.'

Mamma went with the gentlemen to the door, talking as she went.

'The most wonderful thing about violin playing is that you can play two notes at the same time.'

She gave her hand to Lucien first, quickly. How often her hand had lingered in Lucien's! Now it lingered in Obenchain's. She thought of saying, 'You're sure you'll come back?' but she resisted the impulse. Obenchain's gaze was no longer merely admiring, it was adoring.

⁄ At the drawing-room door she halted. 'Only one more piece, daughter, only one!'

'Right-oh!' agreed Marian. 'Now, Alec, step along.'

Mamma stood in the hall. She had no desire to sleep, she wished to talk things over. But Marian did not like to talk things over; even if she waited for her, Marian would say, 'Mamma, I must sleep.' Lee would be asleep already, or pretending. There was, however, some one to whom she could talk, and she walked back to the kitchen. She would tell Celeste that she might have the green dress and she would repeat to her the compliments which Obenchain had given her cooking.

Celeste was finishing the last pan. Just outside the door sat a colored man asleep in an old rocking-chair.

'Waitin',' explained Celeste. 'Mistah Washin'ton Jay. Waitin' since sebben o'clock.'

'I came to tell you the compliments you had,' said Mamma. 'Mr. Obenchain — that was the gentleman from Baltimore — said your cooking was the best he'd ever tasted. He's a very rich man, and he can have everything he wants. He has the great big store in Baltimore.'

'I hear tell ob him,' said Celeste. 'I once got los' in dat sto'.'

'I suppose he's accustomed to the best of foreign cooking as well as American cooking, and that was what he said about yours.'

Celeste approached Mamma with a mysterious air. 'He done mo' dan say it, Miss Mabel. He prove it. He lef' dis undah he plate fo' me.' Celeste drew from her bosom a five-dollar bill.

Mamma saw the amused eyes of Marian, the contemptuous eyes of Lee. She felt that she would defend Obenchain against the world. 'He's one of Nature's noblemen,' she declared.

'Dat's suah jes' what he is,' agreed Celeste. 'I seen dat de moment I looks at him. Men is like hosses; some has good eyes, an' some has bad eyes. Depen's on how much you can see ob de whites. I say to myse'f when I sees dis gen'man, I say ——'

'I wouldn't tell any one about this gift,' interrupted Mamma.

'Not I! I don' eben tells him.' Celeste pointed with her thumb toward the sleeping figure. 'I keeps dis fo' de rainy day. What wages I gits, dat he knows, but dis he ain't goin' to know, not even if he gits baptize'!'

Mamma passed through the dining-room. The table had not been entirely cleared, but that made no difference to Mamma. Nothing made any difference, even the envelopes in her desk, even the recollection of the ticket so carefully removed from her brocade dress — $300.00!

She ascended the stairs and entered her room and took off the beautiful dress and hung it up carefully. She walked to the mirror and stood looking at the image of her faultless arms and neck. Her husband had cared for her body for about as long a time as she had pretended to care for his music and his mocking, learned talk. A hot tear fell on her cool flesh. Time was passing! Time was passing!

III

ARIETTA LEE

I

LEE entered the dining-room with a slow and dignified step. It was exactly eight o'clock, an hour before her usual time for rising, but she was irritated because Mamma and Marian had not appeared. Her step was slackened by feelings of both irritation and superiority, and by inability to move rapidly. The late July temperature, rising for days, had attained an unnatural and most oppressive altitude; besides she was approaching the physical condition of the prisoner kept on fare too meager to support life, or of the wanderer in the desert whose knapsack is empty or whose cache is lost. Black spots danced before her eyes, her knees quivered, her color under the cleverly applied and delicate coating of rouge was that of a person long ill. When she put her angry emotion into words, her voice was weak.

'If we're going to Baltimore to-day, they'd better get up.'

She had waked early and against her will and lay sullen and fuming. First of all sounded the chorus of birds in the trees beside the house and in the fields back of the house — to her a hateful cacophony. Then arrived Celeste shouting to Washington Jay, who had escorted her to her work, shrieking with laughter, noisily unlocking the back door, lifting her voice in a revival hymn, banging the lids of the stove, rattling the dishes.

Having been roused by these sounds, she would have found it possible to go back to sleep had it not been for Mamma. Hitherto Mamma had loved sleep better than anything in the world; at present, living in excitement, she seemed neither to wish nor to need sleep. There was no telling what new attention Mr. Obenchain would bestow. There was now a long night letter which she received with blushes, which she read in private, and which she finally exhibited under pledge of secrecy first to Lee, then to Marian. It might easily have been shown to all the world, containing as it did merely wishes for her good health, and the announcement that Obenchain would spend an hour with Mrs. Young and her daughters. It was probable, thanks to the communicativeness of the telegraph operator, that the world of Bon Air, at least, knew every word.

There arrived also gifts — candy in silk boxes, candy in satin boxes, candy done up in cloth of gold. There came finally candy in the hull of a beautiful boat-model, at the delicate structure of which even Marian exclaimed with admiration. Mamma examined the masts, the sails, the figure at the prow, the tiny crew, and asked at last with awe, 'Fifty dollars, do you suppose?'

'A hundred at least,' reckoned Marian, whose figures were always conservative.

There were flowers which could not be raised in
ordinary gardens, but which lengthened their spikes
under the eyes of experts — gladioluses which
Mamma described as over a yard long, and snap-
dragons of every delicate and lovely shade.

'His own raising, doubtless,' cooed Mamma. To
match the gardens and greenhouses — she constructed a palace, enormous and sumptuous.

There were gifts not only for Mamma but for
Marian — music in sheets, music in bound volumes,
music freshly imported, Scriabin, Palmgren, Juon,
Debussy, Strauss. There was even a night letter for
Marian, announcing the arrival of a new gift.
'Picked up a volume for you in a second-hand shop.'
The volume when it came was two volumes, bound
like a prayer- and hymn-book so that the cover of
one might be slipped into a pocket of the other. The
binding was of finest leather, deep red in color,
tooled with gold. The text was a miniature of the
scores of the Beethoven symphonies.

'But what in the world is it for?' inquired
Mamma, still more delighted than Marian. 'You
couldn't see to play these fine notes!'

Marian was actually pale. 'They're printed this
way so you can follow the music as an orchestra
plays. This is priceless!'

There was music also for Marian to play with
Alec. He had been gone now for two weeks, and he
was to be expected back in another week. Marian
spoke of him at every meal, and, when she did so,

the pain in Lee's heart ceased its gnawing, until Marian spoke just as possessively of Lucien.

For Lee there was a golden chain. Lee said sharply, 'I don't want his presents!' but she put the chain round her neck and there it stayed. It was composed of spheres of finest filigree; she had never seen so beautiful an ornament. There was nothing in Bon Air like this.

'Do you think we ought to accept them?' asked Marian, hugging her music in her arms.

'I see no reason why we shouldn't.' Mamma spoke with dignity and with pride. It was unusual for Marian to ask her advice in matters of etiquette and very complimentary and altogether as it should be. Everything was at present as it should be; Mamma was still like the bride upon whose pleasure all wait. The envelopes were forgotten, the meagerness of her wardrobe had ceased to be a subject for acute worry, the lack of an automobile was not lamented. In certain uplifted moments she believed that everything was to be made permanently right, even to the return of an old glow of the heart. 'I consider Mr. Obenchain a generous and lonely man who likes to play fairy godmother to this old lady and these little girls. I know a great deal about his life. He has confided in me. It has been very, very sad.' Mamma's voice shook.

'This old lady indeed!' Undemonstrative Marian patted her mother's cheek. Marian was perfectly lovely; she seemed to have lost her cool practicality and to have become delightfully irresponsible. She had not ceased to practice — there were times when Mamma muttered to herself that she would go wild.

Mamma had a habit of ejaculating aloud when she was alone in her own room; now she uttered complete and positive sentences which would have astonished her friends in Bon Air. 'It's too bad that there are different religions, but I don't know what we can do about it,' she declared to herself in the mirror over her bureau. 'If there's anything I despise, it's bigotry,' she declared to herself in the mirror over her dressing-table.

Three days ago, while Lee was out, the invitation to Baltimore came in a telegram. Called to Mamma's side, Marian read it over her shoulder. There was nothing niggardly about Obenchain's telegrams.

'Will you and both your daughters lunch with me on Friday in Baltimore stop I shall be happy to send for you stop my car will be at your door at twelve o'clock promptly stop please wire stop kindest regards to all.'

'Twelve o'clock!' exclaimed Marian. 'What time does he expect to eat?'

'My child, this is no Bon Air bus!' laughed Mamma gleefully. 'Remember I've ridden in Mr. Obenchain's car, and you haven't. Luncheon will be, of course, at one or half-past, perhaps two. I think I shall wear my ——'

'You'd better have some sandwiches to eat on the road,' advised Marian.

'Surely you're going too, Marian!'

Marian shook her head. 'Can't go Friday, you know. Too many pupils. If I begin to postpone, they get demoralized.'

Tears filled Mamma's eyes.

'Now, Mother, don't be foolish. You know we need every penny. You and Lee will be enough to dazzle him.'

Mamma demurred, but not very earnestly. Two were, after all, enough. Marian would rather stay at home; she enjoyed herself only when she was banging the piano. Besides, she looked so serious and so mature, she made Mamma seem far too mature. She was not like Lee who might pass for two years younger than she was.

Lee wore to breakfast an old linen dress washed to a pale pink which would have transformed a very homely creature. As she sat waiting the flush on her cheeks was deepened by a natural color due partly to sharpening indignation, partly to the prospect of the drive to Baltimore and lunch at the Bellevue. Surely Mr. Obenchain would take them to no less elegant place! Perhaps there were even more elegant places. Since the dinner-party she had seen Lucien only in the presence of her mother and Marian. She considered writing him a letter, sometimes an anonymous letter. She thought of saying, 'You're making a mistake. Look about for a true lover.' She did not have time for long meditation, for Mamma and Marian arrived speedily, Mamma from her bedroom, Marian from the kitchen where she had been setting the household machinery in motion.

'God bless this food, Amen,' said Mamma almost before she was seated. 'I wonder what we'll have to eat in Baltimore. Lee, to-day you must not simply play with your food. That would hurt Mr. Obenchain, and you must consider his feelings.'

Entering the room, Marian answered Mamma. She wore a white dress which was freshly laundered and becoming, but woefully out of style.

'Fruit-cup,' said she. 'Made of all sorts of strange things, all ice-cold, in a frosted glass. Then iced consommé, slithery and shivery.'

'Which I hate!' declared Lee.

'Eat, Lee,' commanded Mamma. 'He'll order something else for you, darling.' She looked at Marian as if to say, 'Go on!'

'Or smelts with *sauce tartare*, and little tomatoes, peeled and iced, to be lifted by their little tails. And duckling and strange vegetables. And romaine salad, or a new variety of endive. And *mousse*, or *spumone*. And iced coffee. I wish I were going to be there!'

Lee stared, amazed. 'You're going to be there!'

'Why, no, Lee. I said in the beginning, when the telegram came, that I couldn't leave on account of my pupils, and Mamma telegraphed that you and she only would be able to go.'

'Yes, she did, darling,' said Mamma. Lee's face

had taken on a dreadful look of anger and distrust. She grew so pale that the rouge on her cheeks showed in two bright blotches. 'You were at Nellie's, but surely you've heard about it since.'

'You know I give lessons almost all day,' said Marian.

'Lessons!' Lee could not have expressed the unimportance of lessons. 'Lessons!'

Marian flushed crimson — Lee had no right to speak thus of the profession which helped to support her. But Marian held her tongue. In her flush and her silence Lee saw proof of guilt. The evening of the dinner-party they had tricked her, they were trying to trick her again. She and Mamma would be gone the whole day, there was no telling at what hour they would return, and in the meantime Marian would have Lucien. She might invite him to lunch or to dinner, they might be alone in the house all the long hours when Celeste was at her cabin taking her afternoon nap. Marian might even give Celeste a holiday! Lee saw the house for the first time in her life as a place of beauty and magic where two lovers might sit silent, embraced, with throbbing hearts. Her own heart began to throb, then her body to burn.

'I'm not going,' she announced. 'It's too fearfully hot, and besides I have headache. I had headache when I first opened my eyes. If Mamma hadn't been tramping round and round talking to herself, I might have got to sleep again. As it was ——'

'Lee!' wailed Mamma. 'Not going!'

Marian looked up. This was shameful of Lee, but with this strange Lee one could do nothing.

'There was no intention of deceiving you. We thought you understood perfectly. And what possible difference can it make?'

'The difference is that I'm sick,' declared Lee. 'That's the point. That's the only point. That's all that's involved.' She pushed away her untouched cantaloupe and stood up. Tears seemed to well from her throat to the back of her eyes; in a moment they would stream down her face. She managed to say with composure, 'I don't wish any breakfast,' and she departed, through the door, across the hall, and up the stairs.

'Do you think there's anything the matter with her?' Mamma's wailing voice followed up the stairs. Marian's answer was inaudible and Lee was sorry. In her heart she knew that Marian loved her dearly, but perversity made her wish to have cause for still sharper rage.

'I can't go alone!' This cry was tragic; it followed her to the top of the stairs and all the way to her bedroom. Again she could hear no answer. She fell, dressed as she was, on her bed and let the hot tears flow. She heard again the voice of Mamma, and now the voice of Marian as well. Marian's words were distinct, coming as they did from directly beneath the stairs.

'Four, three, eight.' That was little Betty Butler's

number. 'Please tell Betty her lesson is postponed until to-morrow. Seven, seven, one.' That was Roberta Cline's number. 'Tell Roberta, please, to come to Miss Marian's for her lesson to-morrow instead of to-day. . . . You say she's going away? Very well.' That meant a loss of two dollars. 'Next week, then. One, three, eight.' Marian's voice was crisp and clear; she showed no concern for her poor sister lying smitten on her bed. 'I can give the three morning lessons before we go if you'll do a little mending for me, Mamma.'

'I will, oh, darling, I will!' Mamma had come into the hall. 'Don't you agree with me that I couldn't decline now?'

'I don't see how you could.'

'And I couldn't go alone, could I?'

'It wouldn't be very pleasant.'

'You don't think she's really ill, do you?'

'Not so ill that Celeste can't look after her. What she needs is a ——' Lee listened in eager fury, but she could hear nothing. She filled in the word, believing it to be 'spanking.' What Marian really said would have been equally infuriating; it was 'a square meal.' Marian said still more. 'What discourages me most about Lee is her idleness.'

'She'll get over that,' prophesied Mamma. 'Marriage will sober her and train her. It did me.' Mamma concluded with a deep sigh.

Lee rose, listening intently for footsteps, then bowed the shutters and quickly lay down. But they were not coming up at once. She rose again and smoothed her bed. The doorbell rang; she reposed until the slight confusion in the hall subsided. The first pupil had arrived. She slipped out of her scant garments and into her diaphanous nightgown and lay down once more. Mamma was coming up the steps and through the hall, all at a brisk pace. She was at the door, in the room.

'Sleeping, darling?'

Lee did not reply. 'Poor child!' said Mamma, and went into her own room and half-closed the door. She sat down, supposedly to do Marian's mending; she began to hum. 'Um—um—um, um—um—um,' she sang to a familiar air. She moved about laying out her dress, her stockings, her little slippers. She would not make her bed on this great day; she was a queen and a Victoria born to idleness, not Eugénie risen from the ranks. Downstairs began the odious irregular sound produced by Marian's little pupil and the odious regular sound produced by Marian. 'One, two, three, One, two, three!' There followed a still more unpleasant, 'One and two and three and ——'

'"Sweet Marie!"' sang Mamma in time, but a little out of tune. '"Come to me, Sweet Marie!"'

Again Mamma entered Lee's room.

'Lee, darling!'

'What is it?'

'Have you been asleep?'

'How could I sleep?' But Lee blinked — the one,

two, three, one, two, three, had ceased; it must have lasted, unheard, for three hours. Moreover, Mamma was ready even to her hat. Her dress was fawn-colored voile, her hat was fawn-colored, lined with rosy pink, there was on her wrist a fawn-colored velvet bag. In her other hand was a large pasteboard box.

'Celeste will come up every little while to see how you are. You're all right, aren't you?'

'You're really going?' whimpered Lee.

'I really have to go, dear. Marian agrees with me. She's been very sweet about giving up her work. Good-bye, darling.'

'What have you there?'

'My new evening dress,' explained Mamma. 'I wish to have the position of the lily changed and I'm taking it to Louise. I've marked it and they can return it by mail.'

Mamma blushed. Lee saw her drive to Louise's shop in Mr. Obenchain's limousine of foreign make, she saw the liveried footman step out and open the door. Perhaps, sitting in the car, Mamma would send the footman in with a message. She saw Lucie and Pauline and Marie and Evangeline clutching each other on their bench. Lucie and Pauline and Evangeline and Marie would simply die with excitement. Perhaps they would die first with amusement, since the alteration could have been made with a stitch. If only Mamma could drive round to other places, to the 'Hat Shoppe,' to 'Gates and Rath'; then they might cease to persecute her.

Mamma looked down upon Lee, lying so still and slender and pathetic. 'You must eat a good lunch, darling.'

Lee made no answer.

'Darling,' said Mamma, 'I've been giving a good deal of thought to the future. In case Marian should some day marry Lucien, which is not at all improbable, I think it would be only fair if we should arrange that you should receive a part of the large allowance which she has had.'

Lee's heart seemed to turn completely over — she had never experienced so terrifying a sensation. 'What did you say?'

Mamma repeated her foolish sentences, foolish because in the disposal of Marian's allowance she had neither influence nor power.

'Is Lucien going to marry Marian?'

'You never can tell.' Mamma spoke playfully. 'He used to call her his little wife.'

Lee had intended to go into Mamma's room, and watch her and Marian go down the walk to the gateway and thus feed her anger, but now, racked by a new and paralyzing suspicion, she lay still. She had been lying on her face; she lifted her head, turtle-wise, but dared not move farther for fear of causing her heart to turn another astounding and uncomfortable somersault.

'I'm not wearing my ear-rings,' explained Mamma. 'They hurt me a little. But I'm carrying them in my bag to put on before I arrive.'

'The car's here, Mamma! Good-bye, Lee!' called Marian.

Mamma bent and kissed Lee, enveloping her in a delicately scented atmosphere, then she hastened away. She flew down the stairs, humming like a bee as she went. Lee shook her fist — let her dare to sing! The screen-door closed with a loud bang, her laugh rose lightly.

Lee's heart turned no more somersaults, but it beat thickly, as though the flow of blood were impeded. She heard the engine of the car start, and turned over on her back without inconvenience. She sat up, then stepped from bed, and walked barefooted into Mamma's room and looked out the window. Mamma had neglected to close the sash and the entering air was like air in the neighborhood of a fire.

Lee expected that the car would be gone, but it waited at the curb. All the passengers except the footman were within; he stood tall and straight by the rear door. Beside him stood Willie Wright, who carried special delivery letters in Bon Air. Willie and his bicycle leaned against each other, as though each needed support. Apparently he had handed a letter to the footman, who had in turn passed it to Mamma. Lee interpreted to the silent house. 'Old idiot!' said she of Mr. Obenchain. 'Won't he see her in an hour? Perhaps it's to tell them not to come?'

Clearly the letter had no such import. The footman closed the door, he stepped to his own place,

the car moved away. Willie Wright remained, his
mouth wide open, leaning upon his bicycle, his bicycle leaning upon him. In the midst of her woe,
Lee was able to make a cynical observation. 'Nobody'll work in Bon Air to-day.'

Still in her bare feet, she crossed the hall to the
head of the stairs and called shrilly, 'Celeste!'
There was no answer. She went on down the stairs
and into the kitchen. All was safe — far down at
the rear gate Celeste talked to Washington Jay.
She returned to the hall and lifted the receiver of the
telephone.

'Three, seven.' She gave little attention to the
amenities of telephone conversation. 'I want to
speak to Mr. Clement. You say he's not there?
All right.' Her face grew crimson; she proceeded to
tell a useless and foolish lie. She hated Lucien's
secretary, Miss Plumley, a creature with a long face
and straight black hair cut short. 'You're entirely
mistaken, this is not Miss Lee.'

Her voice quivered, she tried to hang up the
receiver, it fell and dangled on its cord. She tried
again, and succeeded. Was Lucien out of town?
Was it possible that he had gone with Mamma and
Marian, and that only she was left? There was but
one way to express her fury; clenching her fists, she
uttered a shriek.

She crept slowly up the stairs, stumbling as she
went. Mamma and Mr. Obenchain! Marian and
Lucien! A frosted cup! The sound of running

water! Distant music! Waiters — how they would watch Mr. Obenchain's least motion! There would be no bargaining or studying of menus such as was necessary for her and Mamma to do — all would be thought out, provided for. Mamma and Marian handed about like princesses by Mr. Obenchain and Lucien! There would be music — lovely 'Humoresque,' romantic 'Marchèta,' played on a 'cello.

'Lucien!' she cried faintly. 'Lucien!'

She sat down by the window, weakness threatening her in an overwhelming wave. She felt a convulsive motion of her diaphragm. People sometimes got hiccoughs and hiccoughed till they died — she did not wish to go that way. Illuminating gas, morphine — they were decent ways of dying, but not hiccoughs. Diagnosing her case at least partially, she called out the window, 'Celeste!' putting so much effort into her cry that Celeste heard instantly, and bade her friend depart. She shouted, 'Comin' fast's I can, Miss Lee!'

'I want something on a tray,' shrieked Lee, still in a surprisingly loud voice. 'And I tell you I want it quick.'

'Yes'm! Yes'm!' screamed Celeste, grinning. She had no faith in the seriousness of Miss Lee's malady — Miss Lee merely had a spell. She yelled at the top of her voice, as both she and Miss Lee did frequently when they were relieved of espionage. There was no Queen Victoria business here. 'What you want, Miss Lee?'

'Cantaloupe,' screamed Lee. 'A whole cantaloupe. And one piece of thin toast.'

'Yes'm,' shrieked Celeste. Celeste delighted in
this weather; full of vigor, she leaped up the walk
like a chamois.

'He won't marry Marian,' wailed Lee. 'He can't!
He shan't!'

II

Lee sat in Mamma's low chair in the sitting-room,
a large fan in her hand, a tall glass of iced-tea on the
arm of the chair. She sat perfectly still, with her
head resting against the back of the chair, and her
eyes closed. Her soft yellow hair curling about her
cheeks, her childish nose, her long lashes, all gave
her the look of an adorable baby, and the bright
spots on her cheeks gave her the look of a baby in
high fever.

The slatted shutters were bowed, but the windows
were not closed as they would have been if Mamma
and Marian had been at home, and the still heat
from under the trees filled every room. The whole
house had the delicious smell of the woods. It had
also the look of the woods, with its deep shadows
and its barred patches of sunlight. There were
other details which indicated that Mamma and
Marian were not at home. The magazines read last
evening lay about, the flowers brought in yesterday
morning had neither been supplied with fresh water,
nor disposed of.

The clock struck two. The sound was shrill, as though the rising temperature made the vibrations more rapid. As the temperature rose, the air changed its quality and became hard to breathe. With the sound of the clock Lee opened her eyes and fanned herself and took a deep draught of tea. On such a day Marian kept steadily at work, and even Mamma was not altogether inactive, wearying herself in the morning so that she might sleep in the afternoon. It did not take a great deal of exertion thoroughly to weary Mamma. Lee had done nothing except rise and dress. She had not made her own bed, and still less Mamma's. Since making beds was not Celeste's duty, they remained as they were, and would remain as they were until the other members of the family returned.

Lee's breakfast served for lunch as well. When she moved, her head swam, and again black spots danced before her eyes. She wished that she had eaten nothing at all.

She had moved several times since she seated herself in the deep chair. At half-past twelve she called Lucien's house. Neither Johnson nor Millie could hear the telephone; if no one responded, then Lucien was not there. No one responded. She rang again at quarter to one, again at one. Still no one answered. Clearly, Lucien was having his lunch elsewhere. She heard again the sound of water trickling from the fountain at the Bellevue, saw a frosting of ice on a glass chalice, heard the romantic strains of 'Marchèta' played on a 'cello with an almost inaudible piano accompaniment. In order to fill full the cup of her despair she went to the piano.

On the piano was Marian's music, an open volume on the rack, a pile of volumes on the end of the bench, another on the lid. She regarded the pile on the bench, and, instead of sliding past, lifted the volumes and dropped them by twos and threes on the floor, happily not on their corners, but on their flat sides — bang! — bang! — bang! She struck a chord, but her mood had changed and she could not enjoy romantic 'Marchèta.' Besides, her fingers were stiff; Marian's hateful prophecy was coming true — if she did not practice she would presently not be able to play. With the flat of her hand she struck a dozen discordant notes at once, and rose.

She passed from the dim room into the brighter hall. As the sun sank to the west it was the Young custom to pull a curtain across the Palladian window at the turn of the stairs, otherwise light and heat streamed in. This at least Lee remembered to do. At the moment that she started slowly up the stairs she heard a step on the terrace. She determined to keep on, and to stay upstairs until the visitor had departed.

The visitor was her friend Nellie Roper, who could not be avoided. She touched the knocker lightly and entered in the friendly fashion in which she and Lee went in and out of each other's houses.

'Lee!'

Lee pulled the curtain and came slowly down the steps. She walked very straight and her bare knees showed between the tops of her stockings and the hem of the shrunken pink dress. She might easily have passed for fourteen instead of eighteen. The black spots had for the moment ceased to trouble her. She carried her head high; independence had its charm.

'Not all alone?' Nellie stood at the door of the sitting-room awaiting her. Nellie had no beauty; she was short and stout, her brown hair was very straight, her complexion was sallow. Her taste was poor; it was certain that she would have a rainbow wedding.

'All alone.' Like Mamma, Lee had quotations, remembered from poems required to be memorized in school. '"Alone on a wide, wide sea." Come into the sitting-room. Mamma and Marry have gone to Baltimore to lunch. It's fiercely hot, isn't it?' She did not return to her armchair which seemed very far away, but sank down on the sofa beside Nellie.

'I hadn't realized that it was hot,' sighed Nellie.

Lee turned and looked at her. Nellie's face was flushed and shining, the homely breadth of her forehead was more than ever apparent under the glistening sheen. But something else in her countenance held Lee's eye, a sort of beauty which did not depend upon beauty of feature. Lee's heart began to throb, color rushed to her cheek hiding the bright spots with a uniform pink.

'I have something to tell you,' announced Nellie.

Perversity and envy and embarrassment held Lee's tongue from crying instantly, 'I know what it is — you're engaged!' Instead she said, 'You look hot, whether you're hot or not.'

'But I'm not!' Nellie leaned forward, clasping her hands. She regarded Lee with the yearning affection with which Marian regarded Lee. 'Oh, Lee, darling, I have something very important to tell you!'

'What is that?'

'I'm engaged.'

'Engaged!' With a mighty effort, Lee made herself appear responsive. 'You certainly have my good wishes. I suppose it's Allen Thrasher.' She did not lean forward to embrace Nellie; in fact she withdrew a little from her. It was too hot for embraces.

'You guessed it!' laughed Nellie. She straightened her shoulders and folded her hands lightly in her lap. She had looked forward to telling Lee everything, or almost everything; now she told her only a few facts which every one would soon know. She saw Lee's motion of withdrawal and felt a new dignity. She had loved Lee desperately, and Lee had often grieved her; now Lee had the power to grieve her no more.

'It's to be on the first of October. Allen's father is going to build us a house. There's plenty of room at the Thrashers' or in our house, but our parents think we should start by ourselves. I came to ask you to be my maid-of-honor.'

'I'd love it!' Lee succeeded in being a little more cordial.

'Our parents had a solemn meeting last night. They all seem to be very well satisfied.'

Lee saw the parents of Allen and the parents of Nellie; the fathers, dignified Judge Thrasher and shrewd Mr. Roper; the mothers, tall Mrs. Thrasher, stout Mrs. Roper, conferring together, discussing ways and means for their children. She thought of Mamma, dressed in fawn-colored voile, gone to Baltimore to lunch with Mr. Obenchain whom she had known for less than two months and her heart filled with bitter resentment. There were ways in which Mamma might have advanced the cause of her child, if Mamma truly loved her. It was not she whom Mamma loved, it was Marian.

'I have oceans of sewing to do. A woman comes from Baltimore to-morrow to plan my dresses. And there are towels and sheets and pillow-cases and a million other things to be looked after.'

With lofty dignity Lee escorted Nellie at last to the door. Her hands shook, her throat was congested. Kind, affectionate Nellie in her place would have hugged her and said, 'Oh, darling! I'm so glad you're happy!' Nellie would have rejoiced in her happiness, but Lee rejoiced in no one's happiness.

She tottered back to her armchair. The ice was melted, and she looked at the tea with distaste, even with loathing. She set the glass on the floor, leaned back her head and closed her eyes. The heat burned her face. When the knocker sounded loudly, she rose without thinking and went to the door. She would fasten the door after she had dismissed this intruder, then she could be at peace.

Seeing a man whom she did not know, she laid her hand on the lock of the screen-door and without making any effort to conceal her motions tried to turn it. But her hand was weak.

'Is Mrs. Young at home?' The voice was sharp, the countenance that of a racial kinsman, however far removed and lowly, of Obenchain.

'No, she isn't!'

'When will she be in?'

'I'm sure I have no idea.' Lee's voice was clear and high; suspecting the man's errand she threw into it a note of impertinence.

'Will she be in to-day?'

'I told you I had no idea when she would be in. Didn't you hear me?' Lee leaned on the lock, feeling her knees quiver.

'Where did she go?'

'Sir!'

'Where did she go?'

'You must be losing your mind!'

'She knew I was coming.'

'Perhaps that was the reason she left,' said Lee insolently.

'That may well be,' agreed the stranger. 'Well,

you tell her a legal representative of Gates and Rath
called upon her and that he'll be back to-morrow.
Other representatives have called upon her, but not
me. I have the authority of the law — get me? Get
the name? — Gates and Rath of Baltimore.'

Lee felt more and more wretched, but she must
show this creature that her wretchedness had nothing to do with him. The black spots which danced
before her eyes turned red.

'I take no orders from Gates and Rath,' she said
shrilly and stepped inside the inner door and closed
it with a bang. The very house shook, the prisms
on the chandeliers tinkled, and lightly balanced
pictures moved from their positions.

She opened the door in a moment to be sure that
the stranger was gone, then she staggered to the
swan's-neck sofa and there sat down. Then she lay
down. The sofa was covered with haircloth which
felt deliciously cool. It seemed to revive her and she
rose and returned to her armchair. If Lucien would
only come now and find her and comfort her! But
Lucien was hearing music and engaging in intellectual conversation and feasting on iced fruit-cup
and fishes in their skins, with peas for eyes — a
great qualm racked the frame of Lee.

The qualm passed. She sat perfectly still, her
head resting on the cushion, one hand laid on the
arm of the chair, the other in her lap. She was suddenly wholly comfortable and at peace. The clocks
struck three, then four. The air grew warmer,

heavier; a locust lifted his shrill voice. There were no sounds but the sounds of summer and the ticking of clocks. The clocks at last struck five.

The next moment Lee woke. She moistened her lips with her tongue. They were dry, and what a horrible taste there was in her mouth! She moved her hand, how very tired she was! The room was dim, and there were no longer any streaks of sunlight on the floor. She remembered all the day's events — Mamma and Marian had gone away and left her alone and she was ill. She might die before they got back. The air was so heavy that breathing was difficult, and the effort to fill her lungs exhausted her.

She heard whispers — it was not like Mamma and Marian to whisper! And Mamma and Marian were in Baltimore, they were not in the house. Celeste sometimes talked to herself, but never in whispers. Was it Mamma and Marian, and were they discussing her? No longer weak, she sat straight, every sense alert.

'Heavenly!' cried a voice which was unmistakably a woman's, but which was deep enough to be a man's.

'I confess I'm a little uneasy,' answered a piping voice.

'Nonsense!' declared the deep voice in a louder tone. 'We can say that we rapped and that no one answered and that we love beautiful things and ventured in. These Southerners are all hospitable;

they'll make us feel at home. Look at that —
Chippendale! And that — Heppelwhite!'

The owner of the thin voice seemed to be convinced. 'I want you to look at those pendants.
Priceless! Did you ever see anything like that
ottoman?'

'Look at those hurricane shades!' The strangers
must be standing now before the hall table. 'I never
saw or heard of such a thing as hurricane shades
engraved with a monogram!'

'Nor I.'

'I ask you to look at that table — Duncan
Phyfe!'

'Do you suppose it's original?'

'Original! It's stood in that spot since the day it
was bought. They doubtless think it's a poor old
thing!' The deep voice took on an hysterical note.
'Did you ever see such objects? Everything could
go into the American wing "as is." To think of them
being here in this out-of-the-way place!'

'They have a fine new piano,' remarked the thin
voice. 'And look in that room at the books! I don't
believe we could buy anything.'

'You watch me!' chuckled the thick voice.
'They're all poor. If I die in the effort, I'm going to
get this sofa.'

The sofa creaked, and instantly Lee rose and
walked toward the sitting-room door. They had not
entered the library, they were walking down the hall.
Perhaps they expected to stop in the library and the

sitting-room on their return journey. She paused at Mamma's desk and opening a drawer took out a small object; then, with catlike tread, pursued the intruders. They had vanished into the dining-room. There was silence, then a sigh.

'I'm dreaming,' declared the heavy voice in a sort of blissful moan.

'Did you ever see anything like this in your life?' The owner of the thin voice asked this question. Neither of the ladies seemed to have an extensive stock of enthusiastic expressions. Lee saw them both — one was heavy, the other light; she observed with disgust that both had short sparse gray hair. They stood as if paralyzed, gazing at the sideboard.

'I want you to look under that table!'

Both ladies bent to inspect the carved feet tipped with brass. The lady with the heavy voice, who was light, bent over; the lady with the thin voice, who was heavy, dropped to her knees. Thus at a disadvantage they heard a shrill inquiry from the doorway.

'Will you please explain what you're doing in my house?' demanded Lee.

Holding the same positions, the ladies turned their heads. When they saw merely a tall child, they recovered enough to stand upright. Their faces flushed and they smiled, apologetically and ingratiatingly.

'Is your Mamma at home?' The lady said 'Momma.'

'No, my Momma's not at home. What do you want with my Momma?'

'We wish to express our admiration for her beautiful possessions.' The lady's deep speech was awkward and stammering.

'You don't even know our name!' cried Lee. 'You've broken into our house! You're curiosity-seekers or worse — perhaps vandals.'

'Oh, no!' protested the ladies together. 'Not vandals!'

'Whatever you are, you will please leave instanter.' Lee raised her left hand. She pointed toward the kitchen door. The ladies flushed; they were ladies, even though curiosity and admiration had made them temporarily forget their manners.

'We've done no harm.'

'I heard everything you said,' declared Lee. 'I heard you planning to buy our unappreciated objects.' Lee remembered a long story of Celeste's. 'I tol' him to make tracks,' said Celeste. 'An' to make 'em quick's lightnin'.' 'You will please,' directed Lee outrageously, 'make tracks.'

The ladies looked at the doorway in which Lee was standing. They looked at the other door which led unmistakably toward the kitchen. They looked back at Lee. Her right hand was hidden in the folds of her skirt. She moved it, there was the glitter of silver and the gleam of mother-of-pearl. The stout lady stepped hurriedly into the kitchen, followed by the thin lady. Outside they began to trot, then to run.

'She had a revolver!' cried the stout lady. Her thin voice grew less in volume and more piercing in quality. 'An old-fashioned, pearl-mounted revolver! I don't suppose it would shoot!'

'Why do you suppose it wouldn't shoot?' demanded the other lady hoarsely. 'Did you ever in your life!'

They hastened to the brick walk, to the gateway. They passed out between the pillars with their graceful urns.

Lee stepped into the kitchen. Hunger has its cruel pangs as well as its enervating weaknesses. She opened the door of the refrigerator — if there were sandwiches made for her supper, then it was Friday and Celeste had gone for her afternoon out. There were the sandwiches; she seized one like the starving creature she was. She ate one, another. Together they amounted to two fair-sized slices of bread.

At Mamma's desk where Mamma sat to write, she now sat down to write. She wrote much the same words — 'dear Lucien,' 'darling Lucien.' She went farther than Mamma — 'Mrs. Clement,' 'Mrs. Lucien Clement.'

When the telephone rang her heart took a somersault such as it had taken in the morning. If Lucien had not gone! If Lucien should say, 'Are you there? Are you there alone?' If he should come and take her in his arms! Then this wretched ache would cease.

'Hello,' she answered, trying to keep her voice low and cool.

'Is this Miss Lee Young?'

'Yes.' No, alas! this was not Lucien.

'This is Baltimore calling.'

Lee clutched the shelf upon which the telephone stood. Baltimore! Surely nothing had happened to Mamma or Marian! 'Hello!' She leaned against the wall. It was not important that she be in a position to speak, she must be first of all in a position to hear. 'Hello! Hello!' Surely nothing could have happened to beautiful Mamma! No one had such a mother as she had. The other girls — 'Hello!' she cried again in a feeble wail. And Marian — why, Marian — if anything happened to Marian she would die. 'Hello,' she whispered. There were crackings in the wire, explained by a low rumble of thunder. She was dreadfully afraid of thunder.

'Lee?' It was Marian's voice, clear, cool, composed. 'We'll not be home till sometime in the evening. Are you all right?'

Lee wished that she had not answered, that she had let Marian call and call. 'Of course I'm all right!' She hung up the receiver. She had made them feel comfortable about her, and she was furious with herself for it.

There was another and slightly heavier rumble of thunder. She was not in the least weather-wise, but the approach of a storm was apparent to the most stupid. She went through the house closing windows, each with a slam. 'In a few minutes I'll be scared to death,' she said in a loud tone. 'Simply scared to death!' On one side of the house was bright blue sky; on the other, soon to hide the sun, was a coppery cloud.

The telephone rang, she stood perfectly still, determined not to answer. It rang again — suppose it should be Lucien? Suppose, after all, he had not gone and had seen the others go and was alarmed about her? Suppose — she flung herself at the telephone.

'Lee,' called Nellie Roper's kind voice. 'Is Celeste there?'

'Celeste?' repeated Lee coolly. 'Why?'

'I thought you might be alone. If you're afraid, come over. And Celeste too.'

'Thank you,' answered Lee. 'I'm not afraid.'

She stood very still. The two sandwiches, small as they were, had slightly revived her.

'I'll give him one more chance,' said she. 'Three, seven . . . Is Mr. Clement there?'

Though office hours were over, Miss Plumley answered. 'Mr. Clement is not here, Miss Lee.' Hateful, presuming creature! 'He'll not be in the office until to-morrow morning.'

'Do you know where he is?' Thus low had Lee sunk.

'No, Miss Lee. And if I did' — these amazing words were uttered boldly, brazenly — 'I would refuse to tell.'

Lee sat on the sofa in the hall; under her weight it gave forth no creak. There was a roll of thunder, slightly louder and much longer than the last reverberation. The storm was still far away, but its method of approach was businesslike; each flash was a little more brilliant, each roll of thunder a little heavier. In imagination Lee heard voices. One was that of Nellie Roper, saying, 'Don't be foolish, Lee! In a minute you'll be scared to death. Come on over!' She paid no heed. Another and inner voice said fiercely, 'Eat!' — but this voice she did not obey either. She had already eaten two sandwiches — a large meal.

She sat herself down once more at Mamma's desk. She tore up the little sheet from Mamma's pad on which she had written Lucien's name coupled with tender adjectives, and took another. 'This can't go on forever,' she wrote. 'I'm not to be fooled forever.' She tore up this sheet and wrote upon still another. 'You needn't look for me. *I've gone for good.*' She toyed with the ancient pistol, unloaded and unused for twenty years. She laid it down, then, frightened by its proximity, rose and walked away.

The storm quickened the pace of its approach. The copper cloud covered the sun, and almost immediately fell dark night. Lee realized that she had been hearing a strange, uncanny whistle. She had heard it before; when the wind blew with tremendous violence directly from the west it produced that

noise in the library chimney. She turned and
looked toward the library. It was a dark room, not
often used. The wind which produced the screaming in the chimney had once blown off the chimney
itself. She put out her hand and touched the electric
button. There was no light — it was the custom to
turn off the current from all the houses when especially violent storms were at hand.

Lee felt many emotions, but queerly none of them
was fear. Wretched, angry, and despairing, she was
not afraid. The thunder began to shake the house.
When the lightning flashed, she could see, in spite
of the bowed shutters, all the objects within her
range of vision. She sat bent over, her hands clasped
between her knees. With each stroke of lightning or
clap of thunder, she stooped involuntarily. The
flashes of lightning and the claps of thunder were
now almost simultaneous. Cutting the heavy
rumble came suddenly another noise, a sharp knocking at the front door which she had closed and upon
which the lock was set.

'Lee!' called a voice. 'Lee!' It was that of Nellie
Roper's father. His hand tried the door. He called
again, 'Lee! Lee!'

Lee rose shakily. She hated Mr. Roper for trying
to help her and she determined to avoid him.
Swaying, she put out her hand. It encountered a
garment with the texture of rubber — Marian's rose-
colored raincoat hanging on the rack. She put it on,
and, finding Marian's rubber hat on another hook,

put that on also. She went swiftly through the dining-room and kitchen, and out the back door.

'I've gone!' she shrieked over her shoulder, and against the cracking thunder. 'You can't find me! I've gone!'

III

Lee stood on the kitchen doorstep, still holding open the door, and listening to the knocker resounding under Mr. Roper's heavy strokes. The thunder, as if it also wished to hear Mr. Roper, or to give her an opportunity to hear him, abated. Her imagination, stimulated to an unnatural activity, pictured the further course of Mr. Roper — having failed to gain entrance at the front, he would come round to the rear. The course of common sense was to re-enter the house and go quickly to the door, as though she had only now heard the ear-splitting knocker.

But common sense had no abode in Lee's despairing and defiant breast; she had determined that Mamma and Marian should return and find her gone. They had treated her cruelly and they must be punished. Just where they were to find her she had not decided. She thought of the stream below the town, and shuddered. It was no part of her vague plan that they should find her wholly dead. To drown and be dragged limp from the water by means of hooks would be as ignominious as perishing from hiccoughs. It was nearer her intention that they should find her dying, along the road, or under the hedge. 'Under the hedge,' as a place to die, was not a term commonly used in Bon Air, she had read it in a story of English life.

Mr. Roper's next thump had a sound of finality — he would now come round the house. There was a flash of lightning, then a roar of thunder. She hesitated no longer, but stepped down to the porch, thence to the walk, and ran toward the gate where Celeste's lovers were accustomed to linger. She wished to make not merely her family unhappy, but Lucien as well. If he saw her helpless and dying, he might pity her and love her and she would recover. She would not recover too rapidly, of course. She saw herself first lying low in her bed with Lucien kneeling beside her, then propped on pillows with Lucien sitting beside her. She wanted nothing of Lucien but his love. What Mamma desired was Lucien's support, and even Marian thought of the comfort of Lucien's riches.

The next flash of lightning and clap of thunder, fortunately for her, caught her at the gate where she could seize a post in both her arms and cling. She looked back at the house; she laughed hysterically — Mr. Roper was standing at the kitchen door, trying in vain to enter. There was a louder crash and a rending of mighty boughs — the violent wind had sent an ancient tree thundering to the earth. Even this warning did not stay her flight. She had no goal, her only intention was to flee, and she stepped out, down the grassy alley.

The sandwiches which she had eaten gave her enough strength to proceed for a short distance at least. She felt elation, both mental and physical. When the next flash and roar came, she laughed again. In a moment she began to feel as though she carried a heavy burden. She did not think of turning down the brim of Marian's hat and in it the rain gathered as in a basin. The coat was heavy, and her slippers were in a moment sodden and heavy also.

She passed the end of their own property and the lower boundary of other wide yards, then narrower yards, then she entered a region of stables. The doors of old frame buildings yawned, and she might have stepped in out of the rain, but she was afraid. She felt now as though she had entered the last stage of life and it was time to select a spot upon which to recline, but she did not choose the dark ill-smelling interior of a stable or shed. Bon Air had few evil characters, but there were a few, and to be beaten into insensibility or to be stabbed to death was, like hiccoughing and drowning, not to be contemplated.

Such an ending once in her mind, it was instantly elaborated by imagination, and in panic she tried to run. She could see ahead the lights of the main street as at the end of a tunnel; she must reach them as quickly as possible. She had thought of turning back into the alley and pacing up and down until she dropped exhausted, but she was afraid to pass again the dark barns.

Reaching the street, she stood looking to right and left. Now she was truly appalled. To hear the wind in the trees round her own house was one matter, to see it lashing the boughs of the wood maples in the center of Bon Air was another. Signs creaked in the wind, the gutters ran full, the arc lights swung back and forth. She looked out into the street and was afraid, and into the black tunnel from which she had come and was still more afraid. In the tunnel she saw a pair of gleaming eyes, and, shrieking, she tore directly across the street.

'Missy!' shouted a voice. 'Missy Mahian, don' you be scared!'

She was too nearly insensible to recognize the voice or person of Washington Jay.

'You better lets me take you home! I knows you' coat. It's a bad night, Missy Mahian.'

Lee was out of hearing. No one could have heard the voice of any human being at a distance of more than a few feet. In another dark alley she leaned panting against a wall.

'I will arise and go to my father,' she said in her soul, meaning not her father, but her home, or Nellie Roper, or Mrs. Roper, or any dear familiar thing.

When she had gained her breath she tried once more to run. Here, too, were dark buildings with yawning doors — the wretch might pursue her and drag her within. At the next cross-street was a gleam of light. She hurried toward it. There she would turn and go back to the Square and then

down her own street toward home. She could easily
explain to the Ropers that she had stepped out and
could not return because of the storm. She thought
of home with longing which almost burst her heart.
Holding out her hands toward the lighted area, she
took a few quick steps. With a sharp crack, a line
of fire leaped from horizon to zenith. For an instant
everything was as bright as day; then, with an effect
upon the human mind as startling as the flash of
light, came entire darkness. There was no longer
even a vague square of light at the corner.

Lee uttered a faint moan. Again she believed that
she heard a step behind her and she dashed forward.
The brim of her hat, unequal to supporting the
weight of water, bent, and a deluge descended into
her neck. She brushed the water out of her eyes and
with it a warmer flood. She was headed now toward
Lucien's house, which could not be very far away.
She would go and die under Lucien's hedge; he
would find her there when he returned from rioting
with Mamma and Marian and Mr. Obenchain. He
would know then what he had lost.

At the next corner she turned to her left. By the
flashes of lightning, now slightly diminishing in
brilliancy, she saw the familiar houses of the distant
continuation of her own street on which Lucien
lived. Recklessly, indifferent to the chance of being
recognized, she hurried on as fast as she could.
Once she gasped, 'My strength will soon be gone!'
There was a box hedge across the front of Lucien's

property; she could easily and quickly find a bed at its base.

Before the hedge, as though some one had tripped her, she fell flat on her face, not from exhaustion, but because she stubbed her toe on an upstanding brick in Bon Air's old-fashioned pavement. She lay for a moment on the grassy border on which her fall had thrown her, then she rose with difficulty, and with her despair transformed to fury. Her foot struck the offending stone and she gave it a sharp kick.

'Darn!' she wailed aloud, stronger words not being the property of Bon Air maidens. To the ears of Bon Air this expletive would have been bad enough.

She saw, as though printed by the lightning on the black sky, a new picture which was an old picture — Marian sitting beside a little pupil, and counting. 'One, two, three,' said Marian with firm authority. 'One, two, three.' She heard Marian counting still more loudly and positively for herself, 'One, two, three! One, two, three!' You could hear the determined sounds when all the doors were closed, you could hear them outside the house.

'That everlasting "one, two, three"!' Mamma would groan.

'What you want you've got to work for,' Marian would answer with set lips. 'Nobody can play for me; I've got to do it myself.'

Lee saw the brown and not very beautiful eyes of

Nellie Roper — how they followed Allen Thrasher, until Allen saw them, and through them to Nellie's heart! Lee saw Mamma looking at Mr. Obenchain, Mamma attiring herself royally, Mamma making her voice like sugar.

'What you want,' said Lee to herself, 'you work for.'

She stood another moment, dripping, then she marched on. She would not kill herself; instead she would go and sit on Lucien's doorstep and be sitting there when he came home. Others, she believed, had no shame about getting that upon which the happiness of their lives depended; she would have none. She would ask Lucien to marry her; if he declined, then it was time to think of dying.

She made her way by the recurrent flashes, each growing less bright than the last. The storm passed, traveling east as though it went to meet the revelers. Now and then she paused and rested. Her body felt at times intolerably heavy and then tantalizingly light. She halted presently to seize a fence post and hold herself upright, but she did not falter in her ultimate intention. She would go and sit on Lucien's doorstep, and when he came she would ask him whether he were engaged to Marian or meant to be engaged to Marian. If he said yes, she would die, simply die, there and then.

Guiding herself partly by sight, but more by feeling, she reached Lucien's gate at last. Beside low wooden posts which supported the gate, the ancient hedge had been trimmed into tall post-like shapes. She felt the tips of the branches and smelled the pleasant bitter odor. Sighing, she stood for a moment holding to the branches; she had, she believed, sufficient strength to get to the porch, but no farther. She stepped from the brick walk to the grass at the side, not daring to trust the slippery surface. It was not so far from the gate to Lucien's porch as it was from the Young gate to the terrace, but the journey seemed interminable. She paused again and yet again, now waiting for a flash of lightning to show her the porch-steps so that she might not stumble upon them. Once she stepped into a flower-bed and filled her slipper with mud.

'The limit!' she muttered to herself. 'The absolute limit!'

In the end she did stumble and fall on the porch-steps. She turned her body and sat down, gasping. Within both body and mind was a great emptiness. She half sat, half lay on the steps until she recovered enough strength to sit up. The flashes, instead of lessening in intensity, were brightening, and the thunder was rolling more heavily. The thunder now proceeded, not from the east toward which the storm had departed, but from the west, from whence it had come — had it, she wondered foolishly, gone round the world? Or was another storm coming? She could not endure another storm any more than a beaten and bruised body could endure another stroke of the lash and live.

Back of her on Lucien's porch there was a swing, broad and long and thickly cushioned. She would not sit on the steps through another rain. In the swing she would be sheltered and there Lucien would surely find her. She gave up all thought of asking him to love her; when he came he would find her dead.

Turning weakly, she rose and climbed to the porch. The house was dark and apparently deserted. Lucien had gone to Baltimore, there was no doubt of that, and he had not yet returned.

The swing hung to the right — no, it hung to the left. She tottered helplessly to the right. She tottered to the left. 'Ah!' she cried with a sob, feeling the seat against her knees. She sat down, she lay down, her body horizontal, her legs dangling. Streams of water dripped from her shoes to the floor. The lightning brightened, the claps of thunder grew louder, longer, more frequent. She saw at last when there was no lightning a faint gleam as of a candle inside Lucien's windows. She rose, she tottered toward the door, holding both hands to her heart. At the door she stood swaying.

'Lucien!' she tried to call. 'Lucien! Lucien!'

She produced no words, but she produced a sound. 'Uh-huh!' said she. 'Uh-huh!' Hiccoughing, she leaned against the wall.

IV

MR. OBENCHAIN

I

OBENCHAIN sat in a deep, cushioned chair in the lobby of the Bellevue Hotel, on his knees a 'Leader' fresh from the news-stand near by. The lobby was large and ornately decorated; the windows were hung with red velvet, the furniture was upholstered in red velvet, the lofty ceiling was upheld by thick columns of imitation alabaster, there was a tessellated floor, polished like a mirror.

At this hour, a quarter to one, the lobby was well filled. Few of the deep chairs were unoccupied, and there was a steady coming and going — business men talking earnestly, cigars in their hands or in the corners of their mouths; stout, middle-aged women in pairs or groups; young girls with young men. Figures, faces, and speech showed half of the patrons at least to be of the same ancient and unmistakable lineage.

Obenchain's eyes were fixed on the floor, and within his area of vision there appeared only the feet and legs of those who walked about on the treacherously smooth surface — feet of men treading surely on broad and heavy soles, feet and stout ankles of middle-aged women treading warily on high heels, slender ankles of young girls tripping lightly.

The day promised to be the hottest of the summer; even within the thick walls the temperature was almost intolerable when the relief felt upon entering was past. There was the tinkling sound of a fountain, and every one hastened in its direction. With it mingled the murmur of soft music — now 'Marchèta,' hated and adored, now 'Souvenir,' similarly regarded.

Not a few of the arrivals glanced at Obenchain as they passed. The whole of his fine head showed against an alabaster pillar and the shortness of his left arm was not apparent; he looked able, interesting, foreign, self-centered, enviable. His suit was dark gray, in the weaving of his black tie there was here and there a becoming thread of garnet.

Though he seemed to stare at the shining floor, he saw neither it nor the moving feet; when he lifted his newspaper, his eyes were blind to the words upon it. He saw through both the floor and the newspaper a portrait of his own imagination. It disturbed him; he drew his fine brows together above his handsome nose, he wrinkled his smooth forehead into deep transverse indentations, he looked troubled and unhappy. He folded the newspaper and for a few moments fanned himself with it; then he unfolded it and held it before him. It was probable that among the throng were many acquaintances, and he wished neither to speak nor to be spoken to.

Again he drew his black brows together, again he contracted the skin of his forehead. The picture

which he projected against space was neither ugly
nor alarming, it was very beautiful and innocent.
The background was a pleasant dining-room, lit
by candle-light, a table spread with beautiful silver
and glass and excellent food and surrounded by
bright faces. The portrait was that of Mrs. Young
in her glory of white brocade and glittering crystals.
The dress was magnificent, but it did not make her
magnificent; it made her on the contrary, softer,
sweeter, more alluring. She sat with her face lifted,
looking now tenderly at her daughters, now sweetly
at her guests.

Obenchain laid his paper on his knees, folded his
arms and looked downward. The background of the
picture changed — it was now the glass and up-
holstery of his luxurious car, traveling in the fading
glow of the sunset. The human subject was the
same — Mamma, wrapped in pale blue, a border
of white fur against her cheek, her arm. The im-
pression was not only visual, it was tactual — he felt
Mamma's lovely left arm lightly touch his own
sound right arm.

Mamma had confessed to loneliness, so had he.
Flushing crimson, he shook his head incredulously.
Suddenly he smiled, elevating one corner of his
mouth; he smoothed out his forehead, he eased his
brows, he rose with a spring to his great height as if
from an engulfing wave. He smiled at Mamma's
confidences; he laughed at his own. No human
woman could possibly be as beautiful as he remembered Mamma to have been!

'I have merely invited two charming ladies to lunch,' said he to himself. 'I'm not in the least committed to anything beyond that!'

It was now exactly one minute before one. The hour was first heralded by chimes in a huge edifice of mahogany and brass, then announced by a note so deep and long that he was able to cross the broad lobby before the reverberation had begun to die away. The lack of symmetry in his arms did not affect his carriage, he held his body in perfect balance and walked well. He had carefully trained himself to this erectness — it held his eyes far above curious and commiserating eyes. He had no vanity in his appearance; when he saw the eyes of strangers fixed upon him, he still believed that they were curious or commiserating. He held his body at this moment with unusual firmness, expressing visibly his mental resolution.

'Nor will I be committed to anything' — he laid his hand on the revolving door — 'ever.'

The door to which he gave a strong push was further propelled by the white-gloved hand of a colored man who had as his only duty in life the pushing of the door. He touched his hat as Obenchain stepped out to the pavement. He knew Obenchain, every one in the center of the city knew him.

'Pretty hot, sah!'

'It is that.' The pavement felt hot to one's foot, the air burned one's cheek.

'Taxi, sah?'

Obenchain shook his head. His eye brightened and the black man followed his glance.

'Heah's you cah, sah!'

Obenchain advanced to the curb. If his thoughts had not been altogether fixed upon his guests, he might have heard the last tone of the clock dying on the hot air. He had directed his chauffeur to be here at one; the chauffeur synchronized time and speed, he arrived at one. The car drifted to the curb, the footman stepped down. Obenchain was before him; he opened the door with his own hand. He was aware of a sense of fullness in his heart, a throbbing in his wrist, a profound curiosity in his soul. It was impossible, common sense told him, that Mrs. Young should be as marvelously beautiful as he remembered her. The candle-light, the sunset, the moonlight, the music had bewitched him.

Mamma placed upon the step a tiny foot, slippered in softest fawn-skin, she leaned upon it the weight of a body dressed in fawn-color faced with rose, she put out a hand covered with fawn-skin — no informality of gloveless hands for Mamma! She laid her hand upon the strong arm of Obenchain and, shifting her weight partly upon it, descended. Her hat drooped a little; she could give his eyes, set so far above her, only a fleeting glimpse of blue. He realized with amazement that he had underestimated rather than overestimated her beauty. A sensation which was neither exactly a thrill nor ex-

actly a chill passed through his body—he had underestimated also the effect of her beauty upon
him.

'We are here!' she cried in childlike delight.

The 'we' recalled Obenchain to himself. 'Welcome, Miss Marian!' said he, holding out his
hand.

Marian had already stepped down. She was
dressed as when he first saw her, in a white dress
obviously made at home — his eye for these matters
was keen — and in a white hat with a red bird upon
it. The charm of Marian lay in her youthful straight-
ness, her dark eyes, her look of worth and ability.

'Have you been very uncomfortable?' he inquired
solicitously.

'We haven't been in the least uncomfortable.'

Marian glanced back into the car — Mamma had
forgotten the box which she meant to take to Louise
— the footman lifted it. 'Do you wish this, Miss?'

'Not till after lunch,' replied Marian. She turned
to follow her elders, they had already been swallowed
by the swinging door.

Obenchain walked by Mamma's side across the
shining floor. Mamma went slowly, steadily, directly. Well acquainted with the Bellevue, she knew
the location of the dining-room and she talked as
she walked. She looked at no one; she was at perfect
ease as though she were advancing from her sitting-
room to the drawing-room to announce to Marian
that she was about to take the long repose which she

called her siesta and that practicing must cease. It was only Obenchain who looked about, to be sure that there was a clear path before his ladies.

Obenchain saw with pleasure and perhaps a little surprise that Mamma was at ease, that she would do one credit anywhere. He saw also — and his face flushed and the smile came now to both corners of his mouth — that she would make one conspicuous anywhere, with the sort of conspicuousness which he loved — that of possessing the best. The tinkle of the fountain grew louder, not only because they were approaching it, but because between them and it sounds were hushed. Obenchain not only heard that there was silence as they drew near; he saw silence in the sudden fixing of heads half turned, of lips half parted. The maids in the checking room stared and the guests proceeding toward the dining-room separated, leaving a space in which he and his ladies advanced.

In the doorway the three stood abreast. The room was long and broad. The fountain was in the center, pale pongee curtains tempered the light, there were hangings of green, there were masses of cool green plants. They waited only for an instant; a head-waiter came forward, another. One nodded with authority. Obenchain smiled at Mamma; she followed the waiter down the long dining-room, her golden head uplifted, her blue eyes smiling, her mouth fixed in its perfect bow. After her came Marian — to her the diners gave little attention, she was merely a step which carried their glance from her mother upward to Obenchain.

Obenchain caught an eager bow and nodded — that was Gulden. He was with his own family, heavy women with every racial feature accentuated. He caught another eye — that was young Gaither with his fiancée, dull, certain to become heavy in body, but not too heavy ever to outweigh her gold. There was — he was so struck by the amazement on this face that he could not give its possessor a name. Mamma had reached the distant corner of the room at last; she sat down in an angle between masses of palms and ferns, Marian took the place beside her, he sat opposite Marian. Mamma looked up, she flushed, he was angry with the staring creatures. But Mamma was not angry.

In the center of the table was a low bowl filled with rose-colored sweet peas and ferns. There were no menus; at each place was set a glass bowl filled with ice in which as in a nest was a smaller bowl of silver filled with fruit. Frost shone on the silver.

'I wish I could lower the temperature!' Obenchain leaned back as though food were nothing, looking at Mamma. His eyes narrowed; said he to himself, 'I will commit myself to nothing!'

Mamma lifted her spoon. Bending her perfect chin, she raised her blue eyes; in them was no coquetry.

'Everything's perfect,' she declared. 'And I'm hungry as a bear!'

Marian lifted her spoon; in the confusion of break-fast she had eaten little.

'You've made every possible provision to cool us off!'

'I tried to do that.' At last Obenchain lifted his spoon also. 'You had, I suppose, no adventures on the way?'

'None,' said Marian.

Obenchain found that he too was hungry. The waiter took away the glass and silver bowls and brought silver cups. The consommé was slithery and shivery as Marian prophesied; she tasted it; it was delicious.

'I wrote a letter to your musical friend,' said Obenchain. 'I thought it might be an advantage to him to play at my house some time in the future. I have a good many musical acquaintances, and they're all talkative. That's the best kind of advertisement.'

'I'm sure he was grateful,' answered Marian. 'Any one as talented as he, and as industrious as he, should have his way smoothed. He's gone to Phila-delphia to play for Bergmann. He was petrified. But I'm not petrified for him.'

'Have you heard Bergmann?'

'No,' said Marian. 'Never.'

'You must attend the concerts in Baltimore next winter, and, if your friend plays for me, you and your mother and sister must come down. It can be arranged easily.' Next winter was far away; the

plans had a vagueness and a boreal chill comforting
to Obenchain.

Mamma sipped her iced and shivery soup from the
edge of her spoon and that was all — her taste in
food as well as in books was old-fashioned. Besides,
her mind was at this moment fixed excitedly upon
another matter. Obenchain had mentioned his
house — there was no reason why she should not
continue the subject. She knew after all only Obenchain himself and his car.

'Do you live in a house?' she asked cleverly. 'I
supposed everybody had moved to an apartment.'

'I live in a house, a house which I remodeled.'
Obenchain hesitated for an infinitesimal space. He
had been made free of the Youngs' house; he could
not in common decency end his remarks here. He
forgot that he had already invited the ladies and
their friends with the most urgent cordiality to see
his etchings, his Whistlers, his Hadens. 'You must
come some time to see my house.'

'That would be lovely!' cried Mamma. 'Is it in
the city?'

'Yes, not far from here.'

The waiter removed the silver cups; he brought,
as Marian had prophesied, little fishes with peas for
eyes; tiny tomatoes, skinned, but with their stems
and calyxes remaining; sauce, yellow and, like the
soup, quivering gelatinously.

'Caught this morning, probably,' commented
Obenchain. 'This dining-room is famous for its

fish.' As though some occult suggestion carried his thoughts to Arietta Lee, he spoke of her. 'I'm sorry your sister couldn't come.'

'We left her in bed,' explained Mamma. 'She has so little vitality, dear child.'

'She's extremely pretty,' said Obenchain.

The stream of conversation did not flow as smoothly as at Bon Air. There was not the coziness of the pleasant dining-room, there were fewer persons to talk, perhaps topics of common interest had already been exhausted. At times, Mamma looked down at her plate as though she were memorizing the pattern. When spoken to she lifted her head quickly, and a deeper color flooded her cheek. Seeing her open her bag and touch an envelope within, Marian wondered whether it was a communication from Obenchain handed her surreptitiously.

'Speaking of adventure!' said she to herself, with an adult's amusement at children.

The little fishes were taken away, tiny fowl took their place.

'Perhaps there's an evolutionary appropriateness in the accepted order of courses,' remarked highbrow Marian. 'Birds are said to develop from fishes.'

Obenchain laughed heartily, then Mamma laughed, her voice like a bell. Two men had sat down near by; the waiter asked them a second time for their order. They looked like men of intelligence and good manners, their contemplation of Mamma seemed to be involuntary, their rudeness wholly unconscious.

Marian's remark reached them and they looked at her with interest. In the recurrent periods of sound and less sound, one of them spoke admiringly. 'Lucky chap!' His voice was lowered, but his tone carrying. It carried to the ears of Obenchain whose heart was warmed. He felt suddenly an immense happiness, as though these women, not only beautiful Mamma, but clever Marian, belonged to him. He wished once more that he might buy Marian a hat, and jewels also, so that she too might be made splendid like her mother.

As though her thoughts were, like Obenchain's, controlled by telepathic suggestion, Marian smiled at him. 'Do you mind if I thank you again for the music?'

'Not in the least! But it was a small matter.'

'Lee wears her chain all day,' said Mamma. 'I shouldn't be surprised if she wears it to bed! She loves it.'

'That pleases me!'

Astonished and a little disturbed, Obenchain saw before him an ice in the form of a bunch of purple grapes, laid on real grape leaves. They had eaten more quickly and talked less than he expected. He could see between the palms and under the green curtains a glaring pavement, white in the sunlight. The air was fiercely hot, hotter than it had been — he could not send his guests back to Bon Air now! Already the waiter was asking whether the coffee should be iced.

'Why don't you —— ' He leaned forward, re-
minding himself that he committed himself to nothing. 'Is there anything to take you home at once?'

'Nothing.' Mamma's mental processes were always accelerated when she was happy and well fed;
she used now an unexpected figure of speech. 'We're
out of school for the day; isn't that so, Marry?'

Marian smiled. 'I suppose so.'

'It's very early in the afternoon,' said Obenchain.
'Too hot for that long drive. Will you not come to
my house and rest for a while?'

Mamma's eyes sought Marian's. Her lip twitched,
she wished so much to accept that she feared accept-
ing would be wrong.

'I see no reason why we shouldn't,' said Marian
pleasantly. 'Will you show us your "Jo"?'

Obenchain blinked. 'Yes, of course!' said he, astonished, then remembering.

Obenchain led the way down the long dining-room
which remained almost as well filled as when they
entered. Some of the guests were newcomers; others
lingered, shrinking from the burning sun and the hot
air. There were not a few who postponed their departure in order to watch Obenchain and his ladies.

In the lobby he left them to order his car. When
he reappeared he came from a telephone booth.
Marian stepped into the revolving door and out,
Mamma stepped in and out, Obenchain stepped in
and out. At the curb the car waited, the footman
beside it. On the seat lay Mamma's pasteboard box.

'Haven't you an errand, Mamma?' asked Marian.

'No, darling,' answered Mamma quickly. 'I've changed my mind.'

'We can easily attend to it,' offered Obenchain.

Mamma shook her head. 'I've really changed my mind.'

The car moved softly; having traveled a few blocks, it turned a corner; having traveled a few more, it turned another into a street of fine houses, most of them old, all of them tall. Before a broad façade of cream-colored stone it came to a halt. The footman stepped down, Obenchain stepped down, the ladies were assisted to step down. An ornate grille slid back, a door opened, cool marble invited entrance. Obenchain led his guests, whether by stepping before them, or by a motion of his hand they did not know, into a tiny, paneled room. The door was closed, the room rose bodily, it halted, the door opened, they stepped out upon a tiled floor. Watching them, Obenchain saw Mamma grow pale and a brilliant light come into the eyes of Marian.

Here also was the sound, not of tinkling but of dripping water, poured from a shell in the hand of a bronze baby standing in a larger shell among aquatic plants. The soft light came from on high — two stories above the baby's head there was a skylight of stained glass — old glass, Marian guessed instantly. To right and left and in front opened large rooms — she saw in a single glance a great piano, a harp, books, the massive furniture of a dining-room, large pictures — copies of Titian, of Velasquez, she judged them to be — in massive carved frames set into the wall, chests, tapestries, all well chosen, well placed, softened either by age or by the dim light.

The door behind them closed; a soft rumble gave place to silence, broken only by the sound of dripping water. It was a strange silence, as of death. Obenchain did not live here, no one lived here! The air was cool, moist, as in a cave.

At last Marian found her voice. 'The genie had nothing on you!' she commented lightly.

Obenchain laughed a hearty laugh. 'It pleases you? Mrs. Young, wouldn't you like to have a room and really rest? And, Miss Marian, you may rest, or play the piano, or look at pictures, or do anything you like?'

'I should like to do anything but rest,' answered Marian.

'Perhaps —— ' Again Obenchain straightened his shoulders as though he were trying to keep his head above the overwhelming wave. Their delight flattered him, made him a little irresponsible. 'But I commit myself to nothing,' said he in his own mind. 'Perhaps' — he proceeded with his sentence — 'Perhaps you'll have dinner with me here and drive home in the evening.'

Again Mamma's eyes sought Marian's.

'We should have to let my sister Lee know.' Marian spoke slowly, her eyes holding Mamma's gaze — why did Mamma look so eager and yet so frightened? 'Perhaps ——'

'You can easily do that,' said Obenchain.

'Yes, you can easily do that,' echoed Mamma. She spoke with a gasp, as though she had been running from an enemy and saw a sanctuary in sight.

'A maid will show you your room,' said Obenchain to Mamma. 'I'll take you to the telephone,' said he to Marian. He pressed a button, the soft rumbling responded. He waved Mamma into the little room, he escorted Marian to the telephone.

'I would like to speak to Mamma before she goes to sleep,' said Marian, reappearing. 'Then may I play?'

'By all means,' said Obenchain. 'Later I would like to show you some things which may interest you.'

Marian stepped again into the little room; manipulated by a maid, it ascended. She stepped out into a gallery and looked down upon the baby among the aquatic plants. The maid tapped for her upon a closed door, a voice answered, the maid turned the knob, and she entered. She was in a luxurious sitting-room, opening into a luxurious bedroom. The hangings were rose-colored, the furniture was upholstered in rose. Upon a rose-colored *chaise longue* lay Mamma in a rose-colored robe, rose-colored slippers on her feet, her golden curly hair spread out upon the pillow. There was a suggestion of the harem in the pointed toes of the slippers and the golden pompons. Otherwise Mamma was a beautiful doll.

'You see I was right,' said she, her voice slightly hoarse. 'Everything's even grander and more beautiful than I expected. There's a marble tub, a rose-colored marble tub, sunk into the floor.'

Marian was reduced to exclamations. 'My soul!' said she in a whisper. She went closer to Mamma and looked down upon her. 'I got Lee in a few minutes. Are you worried about something, Mother?' The address had unpleasant associations.

Mamma put out her hand — her fawn-colored bag lay close beside her. She laid her hand upon it.

'No,' she declared positively.

'Perhaps we should have gone home,' suggested Marian.

'I'm all right,' insisted Mamma. 'The maid fetched this beautiful robe for me and the slippers. It made me a little uneasy. I thought first they might belong to — to one of the — the others.'

'"The others?"' repeated Marian. 'What others? Do you think Mr. Obenchain is a Bluebeard?'

'You can be very silly,' replied Mamma with dignity. 'Mr. Obenchain has been married.' Mamma blushed. 'He has told me of his life. But the price-mark is on the robe — fifty dollars, and the soles of the slippers show no wear. I believe he had them sent up this afternoon from his store.'

'That's very likely. Unless ——' Marian paused,

looking about, frowning. But one did not soil the
innocency of childhood. 'Have a good nap.'

She turned and went out. The maid was waiting,
alert, respectful — surely she was also respectable
and the sign of respectability!

'Speaking of adventure!' said Marian in her heart.
She stepped into the elevator and out. She saw the
baby pouring water from his shell upon the aquatic
plants; she saw the massive dining-room, the great
pictures, the carved chests, the dim library with its
thousands of books, but she saw them only fleetingly
as she passed toward the piano. It was a concert
grand — she had never touched such an instrument.

She sat down — this view was different from the
other, and even more beautiful. The square drawing-room lay on her left, the dining-room before her
in the distance, the library in the angle between. In
the drawing-room were lovely ladies of the English
school — Lavinia, Countess Spencer, smiled at Lavinia, Viscountess Althorp, while Henrietta Frances,
Countess of Bessborough, and the Marèchale de
Muys seemed to listen, the one with amusement, the
other with serious delight to the same speech or
music.

She laid her hands on the shining keys and looked
round the music-room. On the wall above the mantel
was fixed a tall picture — Dædalus binding wings
on Icarus, she guessed it to be. The slender stripped
body of the youth was that of a living being, a light
breeze seemed to ruffle the lifting plumes. She sat

staring till silence fell like a burden upon her, weighing down her shoulders, her arms, her hands.

'He said I should play!' she whispered — muttered, as Lee said.

She pressed the keys, sounding light chords — Chopin, Opus 10, Number 1, to loosen her fingers, Beethoven, the Scherzo, Opus 2, Number 3, to lighten her touch, the Bach Fantasie in C minor to rejoice her soul. She lifted her hands, feeling one with the other, her fingers, her palms, she laid them back on the keys. She listened; the water had been turned off from the fountain, there was no sound.

'If I don't begin, I'll be afraid!'

She dropped her hands, the right moved swiftly up and down, up and down, the left struck resounding octaves. She smiled; 'Good work!' she muttered. She played the Scherzo brilliantly, her left hand as light as her right. She bent to her more serious task, her body swaying. The Fantasie did not look difficult, it was easy to read, but what hours of labor had gone to the production of this smoothness of melody!

'Ah!' said she. 'Not so bad!' She obeyed swiftly a childish impulse. There was no one to see — she leaned forward and laid a kiss upon the shining wood.

In the far corner of the library, Obenchain, seated with a book, watched her. He held his book as he had held the newspaper, for a shield. He rose and began to pace the floor. The rug covered almost the entire surface — it was thickest Ispahan. He walked lightly, but upon it and against Marian's

music the tramping feet of soldiery would have made
no sound.

'What lightness!' said he. 'What an extraordinary memory! What youth! What fire!'

He ceased to put his thoughts into words, his
whole being applied itself to listening.

Marian held her hands above the keys; she
dropped them. There was a Ballade built by
Brahms upon an old song — could she remember?
She tried one key, another. 'Ah!' said she! Her skin
pricked, her face grew pale, her hands struck hollow
chords, they built up a great volume of sound, filling
the rooms.

> 'Why does your brand sae drop wi' blude,
> Edward, Edward?
> Why does your brand sae drop wi' blude,
> Edward, Edward?'

Tragic, woeful, moving — now, indeed, Obenchain might well listen with a solemn delight!

> 'O I hae killed my father dear,
> Mither, mither;
> O I hae killed my father dear,
> Alas, and woe is me, O!'

To Obenchain the music spoke not of woe but
warning. 'Stop!' it said. 'Listen! Think!' He grew
pale, then red. He resumed his walk. 'I've committed myself to nothing,' he murmured. 'Nothing!'

Marian ceased; she sat for a moment quiet, her
mood changing. Smiling, she began a Chopin
Nocturne, perhaps the best beloved of all. This also

spoke to Obenchain; it said, however, not 'Beware!' but 'She is lovely!' He saw his rose-colored guest-room, the rose-colored robe sent from the store for Mamma, Mamma herself on the rose-colored couch in the rose-colored robe. He sat down, frowning, the tips of his fingers pressed together. 'She is lovely!' insisted Marian's music. 'Lovely! Lovely!'

As if suddenly determined to support him in his resolution, Marian returned to her Brahms Ballade, playing it more movingly to the fearful end.

> 'And what will ye leave to your ain mither dear,
>   Edward, Edward?
> And what will ye leave to your ain mither dear,
>   My dear son, now tell me, O ? '
> 'The curse of hell frae me ye sall bear,
>   Mither, mither:
> The curse of hell frae me ye sall bear:
>   Sic counsel ye gave to me, O!'

'How foolish you are!' said Obenchain to himself. 'She cannot be as lovely as you think! You will regret! regret!'

A perverse Marian lifted her hands once more. There was a Brahms waltz, played by everybody. She played it with sentimentality. 'She's far lovelier than you think!' said it to Obenchain. She played a Brahms Intermezzo — Obenchain pressed his hand against his heart as though he feared it might be riven from his side. He remained seated as though he lacked strength to rise. With his sound hand he covered his lame hand. An old emotion overwhelmed him, a consciousness of physical incompleteness, imperfection, a feeling as acute as shame. A profound sadness darkened his eyes.

'Madness!' said he to himself. 'Do you think for an instant she would have you?'

II

Obenchain walked up and down, up and down, then he returned to his book. Again he lifted it so that he might seem to read, but might in reality watch Marian. She ceased to play and sat resting as though for new endeavor. Disturbed, he looked sharply over his shoulder — but there was nothing to disturb! He was conscious of the beating of his heart — it was the silence which made him uneasy. He had constructed his house so that he might have silence, but it had long ceased to seem desirable. When Marian began to play he resumed his pacing, when she paused for a moment he sat down, watching her.

Marian played Debussy — 'L'Isle Joyeuse' was it? — he had given her that. She began 'Jeux d'eau.' Hands and mind became confused, she had not really worked at it. 'Dumb-bell!' she grumbled, angry at her blunder.

Obenchain sighed!—ah! his youth had not anticipated old age in a silent house. He thought of Mamma — not so much of her beauty — it was absurd to be physically charmed by the mother of a grown daughter! — but of her amiability, of her tenderness.

He laid down his book finally, and sat nursing his lame hand. Outside the late afternoon was bright, but inside the light was changing. Above the library mantelpiece hung the 'Surrender of Breda' — the dark colors in the foreground grew darker, the blue landscape lighter, as though a strange sun fell upon the fortification, the verdure, the watery spaces. He commanded the view he had in mind when he selected the picture, he had looked upon it a thousand times with satisfaction and pride, but it gave him now no happiness, it was a dead thing.

He glanced at his watch — the girl had been playing for two hours! He rose and stood a little uncertainly, his cheek alternately paling and flushing. He would like to tell her to stop. He would like to lay his hand on her shoulder and say 'my dear.' Smiling, he crossed the room, the hall. He stood beside her, looking down. She was pale, thin, her shoulders were a little bent.

'You've played enough,' said he, achieving a paternal voice, if not a paternal address.

Marian clasped her hands behind her neck and threw back her head. Obenchain looked into her eyes; she looked back in bright friendliness.

'Muscles tired?'

'A little. I taught all the morning.'

'Taught?'

'Yes. I have music pupils.' Marian's hand moved back to the keys, as though she could not keep away.

'You teach every day?'

'Nearly every day in winter. About half the week in summer.' Marian spoke cheerfully, but her eyes darkened.

'You oughtn't to do that for the sake of your own playing. Somebody ought to stop you.'

'There isn't anybody to stop me.' Marian spoke quickly, her tone sharp. There was Lucien — Lucien was the one who ought to stop her. Was Lucien going on and on, never stopping her? She felt suddenly as though she were old, forty, perhaps, neglected, rejected. How many years was it that she had loved Lucien? 'I do as I please,' she declared sharply.

'Are you ready to see my pictures?'

Obenchain led the way into the library, where on a broad carved desk lay portfolios bound in leather. He brought Marian a chair, lifting it with his right arm alone. With his left hand he pulled on the light and opened the uppermost of the portfolios. He used his left arm deliberately and awkwardly, as though to cease using it were to make it altogether helpless. He brought a magnifying glass and sat down beside Marian.

Marian glanced round into the shadows. 'It can't be night, but it's growing dark! We're like a Rembrandt ourselves, with this bright lamp and the darkness.'

'Yes.' Once more Obenchain was pleased. 'Darkness always comes early on account of the high walls, and I think it's growing cloudy. I hope so.'

There was a faint rumble from without, heard by neither. Obenchain began to lay out the precious sheets. Marian's cheeks grew red. 'I wish Alexander LeConte could see these!'

'He may.' Obenchain lifted the uppermost etching and held it in the best light, a picture of an avenue of dark yew trees against an old house bathed in sunshine. 'This is a Haden. Lovely, isn't it? Here's a Haden after Turner — "Calais Pier." Haden studied and copied other men's work, but that never seemed to make him less original. He was a scientist, surgeon, and artist — a great man. Exciting to live like that, isn't it?'

Marian breathed a choked 'Yes! I should say so!'

'These are by a more famous artist, but not a better etcher.' Passed from Obenchain's hand to Marian's one fine Dutch face followed another, 'Vorsterman, Josse de Momper, Van Dyck himself. There are a greater number of desirable Van Dyck etchings in your hand at this moment than in the possession of any one else on this side of the Atlantic Ocean.'

Great name followed great name from the lips of Obenchain — Hollar, Legros, Cotman, Holroyd, Meryon. From without and above sounded a heavier rumble, like the first, unheard.

'Here are moderns — Brangwyn, Benson. Here's a view of High Street, Oxford, a great favorite of mine. Here' — Obenchain's color altered slightly, his lips quivered — 'here she is!'

This he did not pass at once into Marian's hand, he held it so that he could look at it with her — the head and shoulders and upper body of a woman, flung into a chair in an attitude of exhaustion, her long thick hair spread out.

'Only a few lines; the body is vague; we see nothing whatever of the chair; but look at her! He called it "Model Resting." You may be sure she needed it — anybody who had anything to do with Whistler did. Her name was Jo, she was patient, beautiful, a marvelous model. She ——'

Again sounded a faint rumble, now within the house, heard not by Marian, but by Obenchain. He lifted his head, turned it, and rose slowly.

'I've committed myself to nothing,' said he once again in his heart. 'Absolutely nothing. Your mother's coming, I believe.'

'Yes?' Marian's eyes were still fixed upon lovely Jo.

A door opened, Mamma said a soft word to a servant. Mamma's communications to these servants did not resemble her conversation with Celeste Imogene; to-day Mamma was Victoria herself. The servant answered inaudibly, the door closed.

'Is any one here?' inquired Mamma gently of surrounding space.

'Yes, indeed!' Obenchain's motions were no longer hesitating; he turned with a spring and went to meet Mamma, each still invisible to the other.

Mamma advanced, her feet tapping the tiled floor. Led by the voice of Obenchain, she selected the right direction and stood framed in the doorway. It was possible to open her dress a little wider at the neck and thus to show an inch more of white skin, an inch more of rose-colored lining — she had made this alteration. She had remembered the ear-rings in her velvet bag, they gleamed lustrously against her neck. She had stepped, one guessed, into the rose-colored tub.

Obenchain's eyes burned. Marian lifted her head at last and looked round. She started; she had never yet, though she was her child, become quite accustomed to Mamma. Moreover, she had never seen her look like this, so glowing, so melting. Perhaps it was the background of color and riches which glorified her; she belonged in no simple Colonial house in a quiet village. She seemed to Marian unknown, alien, but speedily Marian became re-acquainted with her.

'Go on with your pictures,' she directed. 'I love beauty, but I don't analyze it.' Good for Mamma! — Marian grinned as a boy might grin. At Mamma's next remark she turned back to her etchings — Mamma looked to her at the moment of this speech simply idiotic. 'I'm not very intelligent,' she cooed.

Obenchain did not find either Mamma's remark unintelligent or herself idiotic. He led her to a sofa and sat down beside her, his blood in tumult.

'I wish you to have that "High Street, Oxford," Miss Marian,' said he. 'I have another. Perhaps it will be the beginning of your collection.'

'Oh!' cried Marian, her eyes gleaming. 'Oh, no!'
Obenchain lifted his right hand. Only in an occasional gesture and in an occasional inflection did
he exhibit the root of his family tree.

'Oh, yes!' said he. 'It's nothing! Nothing!'

'No one ever gave me such a beautiful present.'

'It is my greatest pleasure to share beautiful objects with one who values them.' He turned to
Mamma, protectingly, even possessively. 'Did you
have a good rest?'

Mamma flushed delicately, remembering the tub,
the rose-colored robe. 'I did, indeed!'

'I wish your younger daughter might have been
with us.' Obenchain remembered that he had expressed this desire earlier in the day. Topics of conversation did not come easily to mind — he believed
that it was his own mental condition.

'She is' — said Mamma, and this also had been
said before — 'a little difficult.' Mamma sighed.
'But Prince Charming will come and solve my problem. That's the end of us all.'

'Perhaps she should have opportunity to make
new acquaintances,' suggested Obenchain. 'Is she
interested in that musical boy?'

'Oh, no!' Mamma smiled, remembering how Lee
laughed at Alec's red head, his wild look. She remembered also how fixedly Alec stared at Lee.
Mamma was acute in those matters; she needed only
a hint. 'Though of course she may break his heart.'

'That would be regrettable from the standpoint

of romance, but not from the standpoint of music.
They say genius has to have its heart broken.'

'How very true!' sighed Mamma. 'I believe that
most earnestly.'

Marian rose from the table and asked whether she
might walk about.

'You may, indeed, my dear.' Now the words
came easily, naturally, to Obenchain's lips.

Again Marian grinned, the eyes of her elders being
upon each other. 'May I open doors and look at
books?'

'By all means!'

Marian stood before a golden Titian. Her skin
pricked, her lips seemed to become dry. Music —
pictures — Heavens! how they thrilled one, almost
to the point of pain! She looked closely at the Viscountess Althorp, and the Maréchale de Muys —
here was beauty and intelligence and character! —
at Dædalus binding wings upon Icarus — a singu-
larly appropriate choice for a room where music was
to soar. Alec would approve this selection.

She opened no bookcase doors, but returned to the
piano and played softly, matching in volume the
murmur of voices, making it inaudible to herself,
but not interfering. There were after a while two
interrupting sounds, each louder than the murmuring conversation and the murmuring music.

'Dinner is served,' said a voice.

The other sound was a rumble of thunder.

'We're going to have relief from the heat,' prophesied Obenchain. 'The thunder comes from the west — that's hopeful.'

'It comes from where we live,' said Mamma. 'I don't like storms. Lee doesn't like storms.' Mamma's fawn-colored velvet bag was on her arm; she clutched it as though it too contained that which she did not like.

'No storm shall hurt you,' promised Obenchain. 'And Miss Lee's surely not in any danger!'

'She'll lock the house and go to Ropers',' said Mamma.

Obenchain seated Mamma, then Marian, then himself opposite Mamma. The drip of water sounded once more. Two servants moved about, shod with silence.

'I can't imagine how you got your Van Dycks and your Whistlers,' said Marian. 'I thought they were all unprocurable, finally fixed in museums.'

'There are ways.' Again the slight betraying gesture, the slightest betraying tone.

'Lee never remembers to close the windows.' Mamma spoke a little anxiously.

Marian gave her head a sharp turn. Lee — she had forgotten little Lee! It would be a long day for Lee who had few resources within her own soul. 'Celeste is there, Mamma.'

'I'll drive up with you,' offered Obenchain. 'We'll not linger over our dinner.'

'The thunder's getting very loud,' said Mamma.

'You're not afraid!' protested Obenchain.

'Oh, no!' declared Mamma positively. 'Oh, no! It's really quite dark, isn't it?'

'It seems so.'

The rain descended in torrents upon the skylight in the court.

'It will soon be over,' promised Obenchain, as though the weather were his servant. He smiled at Mamma, a brave adult reassuring a frightened child.

'It's really very heavy.' Mamma was quite right — the storm-center, moving slowly eastward from Bon Air, gained rather than lost intensity.

'I'd like to know about all your paintings,' said Marian in a loud tone.

'I'd like to tell you,' answered Obenchain. He gave reasons for his selections, they were favorites to begin with, and all had to be measurably appropriate to his Spanish background. 'I found the best copyists — some are done by our leading painters. One man can copy Velasquez, another can do nothing with him.'

'That last crash was not so loud,' said Mamma.

Obenchain smiled. 'It will soon be over, I'm sure.'

Mamma was right, the thunder was becoming less deafening, the rain was growing less heavy. A faint brightness lit the stained glass.

'We shall have a beautiful sunset,' predicted Obenchain. The light in his eyes was no longer a bright piercing gleam, it was a beneficent glow. 'I quite long to see your lovely house again.'

'Are you really coming with us?' asked Mamma with delight.

'I really am,' answered Obenchain with equal satisfaction.

There was this time no footman to open the door of the car; Obenchain opened it himself. There was no sunset, or sign of sunset; the gleam of light had been short-lived. The sky was overcast, the air heavy, the street a dim canyon. The gutters were filled, at the corner near by a whirlpool covered the entrance to the sewer. The electric lights came on suddenly.

'There has been a tremendous rainfall.' Obenchain was amazed. 'I've never seen such a volume of water in this street.'

He put Marian into the car, then Mamma, then stepped in beside them. The seat was broad; though Mamma was broad, there was no crowding. He kept carefully apart from Mamma — it was natural that a physically perfect creature should resent physical deformity with her body, even if she tolerated it with her mind and heart.

'You feel that you must go? I could so easily put you up.'

'Oh, we must go!' answered Marian quickly. 'My sister has been alone all afternoon. Unless it isn't safe.'

'It's safe,' said Obenchain.

The chauffeur drove slowly to the next block and stopped. Obenchain peered over his shoulder.

'A tree down,' said he. 'We'll have to change our route.'

'There must have been a mighty wind!' said Mamma.

With caution they moved on. Obenchain showed no anxiety; he leaned back talking; Mamma too seemed reassured. Marian studied the back of the chauffeur — it was remote, impassive, expressing nothing. She leaned to one side, peering into the mirror which reflected his face — he was alert, frowning, intent. There was a bright flash, the reflection of his eyes was green like the reflected light from the eyes of a cat.

'Is there to be another storm?' inquired Mamma.

'That was the aftermath of the storm,' explained Obenchain.

There was another flash, lurid rather than bright.

'I've heard people say that you're perfectly safe in a car.' Mamma's gentle remark was a question, not a statement.

'Safer than anywhere else in the world,' answered Obenchain positively. 'You see' — whether he moved a little closer to Mamma, or she to him, it would not have been possible to say. He felt her arm against his own; he remembered her arm in candle-light, round, white, plump, tapering to a beautiful wrist. He felt a heart-warming gratitude for her complaisance, her sweetness. 'You see we're insulated from the ground by these ——' His voice became unsteady, he lost the thread of the exposi-

tion upon which he was embarked. 'Lightning fol-
lows the path of least resistance, it ——'

'I see,' said Mamma when unaccountably he
paused.

The car moved more rapidly; they left the close-
built streets for a suburban district; they were presently in the open country on the road upon which
the bus traveled back and forth. Mamma was for a
while at ease, but when the flashes brightened and
the grumble rose to an ominous growl, threatening,
terrifying, a shiver passed up and down her arm. It
communicated itself to Obenchain, whose arm,
crippled as it was, did not lack sensitiveness. She
uttered a little whimper.

'There really isn't any danger,' said Marian in her
cool voice.

'If you're afraid, we'll stop,' offered Obenchain.

'No,' shuddered Mamma. 'I think we'd better
keep moving.'

It was certain that they were advancing toward
another storm and that the storm was advancing toward them. It was certain also that Obenchain and
Mamma advanced a little toward each other. The
flashes of lightning were as frequent and constant as
Roman candles sent up from the same stick. The
thunder became a continuous roar, heard distinctly
above the sound of the engine which was driven
rapidly as though the chauffeur thought it possible
to reach Bon Air before the floods descended.
Mamma closed her eyes, and put both hands over

her ears. The car came suddenly to a halt. Before them were lights from cars and from moving lanterns, visible for an instant, then blotted out by lightning. The chauffeur opened the window.

'What's wrong?' he called.

A lantern came toward them. Obenchain lowered his window.

'Bridge down. We had a cloudburst and a tornado up here.'

'Is there any other way to get to Bon Air?'

'Yes, sir, the back road, round by Schletter's. Ten miles farther. It's the only way.'

'I know that road,' said Marian quickly.

'You think we hadn't better go back?' asked Obenchain.

'We ought to get home,' said Marian. 'My little sister ——'

'Then we'll go home,' said Obenchain positively and cheerfully. 'But you mustn't be alarmed about your sister. You have a servant, and there are neighbors, and there's Mr. Clement.'

'I know,' said Marian. 'There isn't any reason to be worried. But I think we ought to get home. I wonder if I might sit in front with the chauffeur. I know the road — there's a one-way bridge; you come on it suddenly.'

'Surely, if you wish!'

Obenchain started to rise. The car slanted a little and Mamma unintentionally pressed against him, so that rising was difficult. Marian had opened the door unassisted and stepped out and in beside the chauffeur before Obenchain could lay his hand on the latch. The sound of whistling wind entered and was again shut out. The chauffeur touched his cap.

'What time is it?' asked Mamma.

Obenchain bent forward so as to see the clock on the dashboard. The intermittent thunder was lost in the steady thunder of the rain. 'It's long past ten!' said he, amazed.

'It is!' said Mamma softly. She did not move away; still, though there was so much room, her gentle arm pressed Obenchain's. He heard again the sound of music — 'Why does your brand sae drop wi blude, Edward, Edward?' 'I commit myself to ——' Thank Fortune! there was still light, saving light, shining from the lamp beside the clock, passing between the shoulders of Marian and the chauffeur upon Mamma and himself.

'This is farming country,' called Marian. She spoke in a loud tone, but her voice seemed to come from far away. 'There are fewer trees than on the other road, it's much safer.'

'Yes,' said Mamma faintly. 'Yes,' said Mamma again, the essence of fear in her voice.

'I commit myself' — Obenchain fixed his eyes upon the clock, upon the light. But there was in another instant no light. The chauffeur turned out the lamp on the dash. He bent forward, Marian bent forward. His head remained fixed against the vague gleam cast through the rain upon the shining road; Marian's was now fixed, now turned toward him. They were watching, consulting. The car crept, in second gear, in first, on a road washed into gullies.

Obenchain had no anxiety about the road or the driver. He sat with Mamma close beside him in a box, padded, framed in glass, a sort of lethal chamber. The sound of all things became dull, a spell enveloped him; he remembered no music, neither warning nor inviting, he recalled no firm intentions of his mind. Nor did he remember any excuse of loneliness, of ennui, of paternal longings. He was aware only of the beating of his heart — it was a long time since his heart had seemed to leap from his side!

'I shall commit' — saving words were those; he formed them with his lips.

'I'm a little cool,' confessed Mamma. 'The air is changing.'

Obenchain leaned forward, feeling for the light blanket which should be hanging on the rail. It was there, he drew it toward him. A recollection came vaguely into his mind, foolish sentences heard in his boyhood, not heard since — 'Nobody loves me! My hands are cold!' 'Your mother loves you and God loves you, and you can sit on your hands.'

He did not bid Mamma sit on her hands. He folded the blanket round her, round her knees, her arms, her shoulders. Mamma did not shrink, either from his poor arm or from his bearded cheek.

'I'd like to take care of you always,' he murmured.

'I've been very, very lonely,' whispered Mamma, consenting.

The car slackened its slow speed; the chauffeur changed his gear once more. Obenchain sat straight and facing forward. Mamma moved a little away from him.

'This must be the bridge,' said Obenchain.

The chauffeur blew his horn loudly. The bright lights shone into the black opening of a covered bridge. On the other side a car waited their passing, its lights dimmed. They rose to the bridge, descended on the other side. The car was a roadster, long, low, and gray.

'What kind of car is that?' asked Marian.

'A Horder Eight, Miss. Very powerful. This year's model.'

'I have a friend who has a car like that, but blue and last year's model.' Marian sat silent, troubled. The car suggested uneasy thoughts of Lucien. Lucien delayed, postponed. She had treasured the memory of his handclasp; she was older now, she knew how little it might signify. Why did he not say then, 'I love you — will you marry me?' She moved uneasily, recalling the moonlight, the glorious trees, the enchanted house, the enchanted night.

'The Horder's about the fastest safe roadster there is,' said the chauffeur. 'She'll stick to the road at eighty. She's the traveler! She's the car if you

172 WHAT EVERYBODY WANTED

want to be now here, now there — in New York, say, and back in Baltimore by morning, and not a soul any wiser.'

The rain descended in torrents, the wind blew furiously, the chauffeur shut off his power. 'We're just as far now as though we were starting from Baltimore.'

'Yes,' answered Marian vaguely. She folded her arms, pressing her hands to her sides, unable to think of anything but Lucien. She had thought of the speed of Lucien's car as about thirty; it was queer to realize that it was eighty, and that he might be now here, now there — in New York at night, for instance, and back in Bon Air by morning! She remembered stories — she knew but few, but they were sufficient to alarm — of married men with extra, illegal families, of bachelors with unsuspected offspring suddenly discovered.

The rain poured, then slackened. The car moved slowly. Marian turned on the light and glanced at the clock and turned the light off.

'It's nearly twelve!'

'Yes, Miss.'

Obenchain held Mamma's hand under the blanket. He expected each moment to feel dismay, alarm, regret. He felt none. He expected each moment that Mamma would withdraw her lovely body from its close pressure against his side. Mamma did not withdraw; Mamma, instead, laid her lovely head upon his shoulder. They traveled on and on, still very slowly on the deeply rutted road, the thunder, the rain, the lightning dying away.

'I've been very, very lonely,' mourned Mamma yet again. 'I've had no real companionship. I've had many, many problems. Everything in life has seemed like dust and ashes.'

Obenchain bent his head, again his lips touched Mamma's cheek, her lips. He uttered a faint sound, half moan, half groan, which had, however, no suggestion of grief or woe. He put his left arm round Mamma, his right also; he confided to her all that he had not yet confided.

As though it had endured all that could be asked of a car, the car suddenly wavered in its course. Its motion grew unsteady, it stopped. The chauffeur opened the door and stepped to the running-board, thence to the deep clay. He became wholly invisible.

'Is he — he's not going to hold us up!' gasped Mamma.

The chauffeur returned, opened the rear door, and spoke to Obenchain.

'Flat tire, sir,' said he grimly.

'Indeed!' answered Obenchain vaguely. 'Is that so!'

III

'Mr. Obenchain ——'

Mamma and Marian stood in the hall. The clocks were ticking, there was no other sound. The car was gone, Obenchain was gone. Mamma stood motionless, idle; Marian had removed the hurricane shades and was lighting the tall candles. The electricity, having been turned off, had not been turned on — probably, in the fashion of Bon Air, it would remain turned off for many days. Mamma's hat was awry, Marian's was straight upon her head. The flaring light sent a shadow of the red bird against the wall — it fluttered to the ceiling and perched there, huge, distorted, ominous.

The hall was as it had been. There was no lingering breath of disturbance from the fury of successive tempests, from fright in the breasts of strange, intruding ladies, from strife between Lee and the representative of Gates and Rath, from strife and anguish in the breast of Lee. In the library wall lived a colony of wood-ticks; when it was very quiet you could hear them — you could hear them now.

Obenchain had gone back to Baltimore, traveling cautiously in his great car. Sometimes on night journeys, when the footman was absent, he sat with the chauffeur, but now he sat alone in the rear. In reality he was still in Bon Air.

'Mr. Obenchain ——' began Mamma again.

Marian passed one of the candles to Mamma, and took the other in her hand. The black image fluttered down from the ceiling and settled for a moment on the wall.

'You'd better go right to bed, Mamma.'

The candle in one hand, her box in the other,

Mamma started up the stairs. She looked back at
Marian in an aimless way.

'You and Lucien ——' she began vaguely.

'Mamma, do you hear, it's four o'clock?' Marian
seemed to have reached the end of patience.

'Mr. Obenchain ——'

Marian stepped into the dark drawing-room, into
the dim sitting-room, into the black library. 'This
house is queer,' she declared. 'It's hot and steaming.
It hasn't been opened since the rain.'

'Mr. Obenchain ——' Mamma was now halfway
up the steps. She held out the pasteboard box, as
though depending upon it to utter some vague message for itself.

'You didn't have your dress fixed!'

'Marian,' said Mamma solemnly, 'this dress is to
mark the beginning of a better life.'

Marian started up the stairs. Mamma was compelled to advance or be trodden upon.

'How so?'

'There was no reason to take it back to Louise,
only pride. I can change that water-lily myself. I
will change it myself.'

Mamma advanced into the upper hall. Here, also,
the air was heavy. On the landing Marian undid the
fastenings of the Palladian window and opened it
wide. There entered the heavy perfume of the
woods, of black, ancient earth, of decaying leaves,
and a strange, delicate scent of oak foliage.

'Ah!' Marian spoke wearily yet lightly. 'Ah!

Let us go to bed, Mamma. It will soon be day-light.'

Mamma stepped over her threshold. Here were other scents, perfumes, sachets, scented powder, scented bath-salts.

'I've been very unhappy,' she sighed.

'Unhappy!' echoed Marian from the hall. 'What has made you unhappy?'

'Unhappy,' insisted Mamma. 'You don't know everything that's happened, Marian. This morning before we left I had a very great shock.'

Marian came to the doorway; she held the candle low, she looked pale. The sash of the Palladian window, swinging inward, had set her hat awry, the black image perched on the lintel above her head.

'What on earth is the matter?'

From her velvet bag Mamma took a letter, worn with handling. She held it out to Marian, who set down her candle and read. Gates and Rath declared themselves compelled to take drastic measures to collect from Mamma the final payment for her last winter's coat. A legal representative would visit her and he would insist upon seeing her.

'"Drastic"!' repeated Mamma. 'It says "drastic"! And a "legal" representative. As though they threatened arrest! It is insulting. Will you help me, Marian? For the last time? For the sake of Mr. Obenchain?'

Marian drew her brows together. Her hat, now entirely unbalanced, slid still more to the side. 'Yes,

I'll help you,' she promised, as though, however, helping were not easily contrived. 'But what has Mr. Obenchain to do with it?'

'I don't wish to involve him,' explained Mamma with quivering lips.

Marian sighed — Mamma was trying. She walked about, listening to Mamma's vague discourse. Its subject was Obenchain, his generosity, his nobility, his riches, his good taste — she was a little weary of Obenchain. She opened the door into Lee's room. From western windows a cool wet wind blew upon her. She was instantly aware of something unnatural. Approaching the bed, she laid her hand upon it. The bed was empty of human occupant, but soaked with wet — pillows, mattress, sheets.

For an instant she stood still; then she went round the bed and lowered the windows. She stepped upon one object — that was a magazine; then another — that was a brush; another — that was something round, probably Lee's powder box. Truly the winds had had their way! The floor was wet; the table and chair and bureau were wet. Through all the storm Lee's windows had been open. Lee was always heedless and sometimes mean, but she would not be either so heedless or so deliberately mean as this!

Marian stepped back into Mamma's room, her brows drawn close together.

'Mamma,' said she quietly, 'Lee is not in her bed.'

Upon her own bed, Mamma sank down. She made an astonishing reply. 'Then,' she shrieked, 'he has killed her.'

Without paying heed to Mamma, Marian lifted her candle and started through the house.

'Don't leave me, Marian!' begged Mamma.

Making no answer to this plea, Marian went on again, into Lee's room, into her own room, the guest-room, the bathroom. She looked into closets, behind doors, she peered under beds. She glanced toward the third story, then descended the stairs. She explored the dining-room, the kitchen — Lee was not there. Lee was not in the house — there was no living thing in the house except wood-ticks.

She walked the length of the drawing-room; she entered the sitting-room. She saw on the floor Lee's tall glass, half filled with tea. Her glance fell upon Mamma's desk; starting, but uttering no sound, she walked steadily across the room. On the papers lay the ancient pistol, beneath it writing in a childish hand.

'You needn't look for me,' said Lee. '*I've gone for good.*'

'I thought' — Mamma stood in the doorway. 'I thought — Mr. Obenchain — I tell you he has killed her!'

'Who has killed her!' demanded Marian furiously. 'What are you talking about? In the name of sense, Mother!'

'The legal representative of Gates and Rath.'

Mamma's eye fell at last upon the pistol. 'Oh!' shrieked Mamma. 'Oh! Oh!'

'What nonsense!' Marian pressed her clenched fist upon her heart. She leaned against the desk, the sharp edge of the dropped lid pressing into her thigh. She saw not the ancient pistol but a long gray roadster waiting at the one-way bridge; not Lucien's, but one which reminded her of Lucien. She stared as though it stood before her; then vague impressions, recollections of unimportant incidents followed one another in her mind — Lee's savage irritability, Lee's eyes upon Lucien, Lee's unaccountable refusal to go to Baltimore. Her tired brain tried to explain one fact by another, to find connecting links between small events now half forgotten. Meanwhile through her heart there passed with each breath a stabbing pain.

'It's impossible!' said she. 'Impossible!'

Mamma sank down upon a chair. ''Phone Mr. Roper!'

'No,' said Marian.

'Get Lucien!'

'No,' said Marian.

Marian turned her head sharply. She lifted the nearest shade. The rectangles framed by the windows and barred by the slats of closed shutters were gray instead of black. Soft shapes of boughs and shrubbery were visible.

'It's daylight,' said she, at the same instant that there came a loud knocking at the door. A voice called 'Marian!'

'It's dear Lucien,' gasped Mamma. 'He'll help us!'

'It's Mr. Roper,' corrected Marian.

Marian opened the door, and Mr. Roper stepped in, a short, thin man with a long nose. His hair was disordered, his lean neck showed above a collarless shirt, he held his coat close about him as though to conceal some disarray beneath. Marian regarded him solemnly; he regarded Marian solemnly, her candle, her red bird. He regarded Mamma, who in the doorway of the sitting-room held her letter in her hand.

'You've been storm-stayed, I suppose,' said he.

'We have, indeed!' said Mamma. 'Two storms and two flat tires. You never heard of such misfortunes. And now we've come home to find ——'

'You've had a storm also.' Marian spoke loudly in rude interruption of Mamma.

'A storm!' mocked Mr. Roper. 'Three at least, counting two smaller storms as one. Wind, thunder, lightning — fearful!'

Mamma tried to step in front of Marian; Marian succeeded in preventing her. Surely Mr. Roper had come to tell them that Lee was with Nellie!

'I thought you'd be anxious about Lee,' said he.

'No,' said Marian. 'We supposed, of course, she'd go to your house.'

'Well, she didn't,' snapped Mr. Roper. 'When the storm — the first storm, that is — began, Nellie urged her to come over and she wouldn't. Then I

tried to persuade her and she wouldn't let me in —
that is, I couldn't get any answer. I called and
called, then I tried the doors, and they were locked.
After the second storm, Celeste came to our house,
and with her a colored man. He said you, Miss
Marian, had been running through the alley, but
it must have been Lee, and hè was worried and followed you to Lucien Clement's. He saw you go in
and he knew it was all right. He knew you, he said,
by your red coat.'

'She borrowed it!' cried Mamma. 'She often
borrows things. That's what happened!' Mamma
burst into tears. 'It's all right — Lucien will take
care of her. Millie's there and Johnson's there
and ——'

'We're very much obliged to you,' interrupted
Marian steadily. 'You've been very kind.'

Roper laid his hand on the knob. 'Yes,' said he,
not in any self-laudatory agreement, but because
'yes' was his answer to all questions and his con-
clusion to all conversation.

'Will you go back to bed and get your rest?' asked
Marian, in concern.

'Yes,' he promised.

Marian looked round the hall. They stood, she
and Mamma, where they had stood a half-hour ago.

'We must go to bed,' said Mamma, starting up the
stairs, her candle in her hand. 'Come, Marian!
We're intact — let's be glad of that. I've lost an
ear-ring, but the pair cost only fifty cents.'

Marian waited until Mamma reached the upper hall, until she entered her own room. She then went up swiftly, past Mamma's door. She closed her own door, and raised the windows and bowed the shutters. The light was no longer gray; it was shot with golden streaks, spreading upward and outward from one center, an iridescent corona. She did not wish to see the golden streaks, they hurt her eyes and her heart; she closed her eyes, and continued by the sense of touch alone.   ..

Her room was not like Mamma's, luxurious and perfumed, or like Lee's, pretty and untidy; it was bare, neat, austere. The curtains were white, not rose or blue; there were a few pictures and a few books. When the room was darkened, she lay down, still dressed, upon the bed, her object not repose but mental concentration. As she did so, the red bird, leaving its perch at last, bounded to the floor. She lay prone, her face pressed into the pillow. She heard the door open.

'Marian, dear,' said Mamma. 'Are you there?'

'I am here.' Without lifting her head, Marian saw Mamma, portly but still beautiful — in samite, in blue slippers, a blue scarf on her shoulders, her golden hair spread out upon the blue scarf.

'I wanted to say just one more thing, Marian — that is, how fortunate we didn't have to speak to Mr. Obenchain!'

Marian sprang to a sitting posture.

'Mr. Obenchain, Mother!' she cried fiercely. 'Why this continual harping on Mr. Obenchain?'

'Because he's to be a father to us,' announced Mamma. 'He had and lost two wives and two infants. He's very, very lonely. Lie down and I'll tell you all about it.'

Mamma entered; she sat down by Marian's bed.

V

LUCIEN

I

LUCIEN CLEMENT paced up and down, up and down his brick walk. He held his fine head high, as was his habit, though both physically and mentally he was depressed. It was only Tuesday, but the record climb of the thermometer, which was to reach its apex in storm and tempest on Friday, had begun. The temperature even at twilight was above ninety and the air was motionless.

Lucien would have been more comfortable sitting on his porch or lying in his swing, but he felt that he must court sleep by exercise. All day he had been in his office in the Square, and there under the thick foliage, the unstirred air was heavy. The immediate air was scented by a perfume worn by Miss Plumley, which was sometimes fresh and sometimes stale, but always present, Miss Plumley believing that constancy to a single perfume indicates originality and distinction in taste.

Miss Plumley was invaluable, but she was at times very tiresome. She knew all Lucien's business affairs, which was necessary and inevitable, and she knew also all his private and personal affairs, which, indeed, any one might know. He thought of her as a perfectly efficient machine; he did not understand

that no human machine is perfect unless it is moti-
vated by affection. That Miss Plumley might be in
love with him he did not suspect; though she had
been in his employ for ten years, he had not looked
at her either long enough or directly enough to gauge
her feelings. He observed vaguely that her body
was short and broadly built, that her face, on the
contrary, was narrow and very pale, and that its
length and its paleness were accentuated by lines of
black hair hanging straight on each side; but of her
heart and soul he took no note.

Lucien might have occupied his mind with reading. He had opened a book after dinner, a biography
of Disraeli, interesting and well-written, but had
closed it, unable to fix his attention upon the words.
His thoughts were with his friends at the opposite
end of Bon Air, and his heart was sore. He understood that Mamma's grasp had grown less warm,
her eye less ardent. He saw clearly who now had her
warm clasp and her bright glance. He had long ago
given up all idea of marriage with Mamma, but that
made him no happier about the prospect of her
marrying Obenchain.

He was even more weary of Obenchain than he
was of Miss Plumley. When Obenchain was not
present in the flesh, he was the constant subject of
eulogy.

'Our good friend was here last evening,' Mamma
would say as though she had but one good friend.
'Our good friend has remembered us again.' She

would display a magnificent box of candy. 'Our good friend is coming to-morrow.' 'Our good friend has invited us to lunch with him in Baltimore on Friday. Marian cannot go, but Lee and I are going.' She had looked at Lucien inquiringly — no, our good friend had not invited him.

Worst of all, even Marian, lovely and desirable, offended. 'Here, look at this music, Lucien! It's too exciting — all these things, that I knew of, but I didn't suppose I should ever possess. Imported! Frightfully expensive!'

'I thought you disliked modern music.'

'I was an idiot,' laughed Marian. 'I frequently am. Come, listen!'

Lucien obeyed unwillingly. He found the compositions strange, cacophonous, discordant, incomprehensible.

'Thrilling!' declared Marian, without asking for his opinion.

At Lee he did not glance, of Lee he did not think; if he had he might have seen a comforting reflection of his own dislike. When Obenchain was present, Lee absented herself, or sat glowering in a corner.

Even Celeste Imogene, with whom he had hitherto been a favorite, had transferred her devotion. If he saw Obenchain's car at the curb, he went no farther; but sometimes the car had driven away, leaving Obenchain undiscernible within. Then Celeste opened the door with a flourish, dangling earrings in her ears, a smile upon her face.

'He's heah!' she would announce in a loud whisper. 'He's in de sittin'-room fascinatin' de ladies.'

Now and then, promenading in the warm night, Lucien paused between the boxwood pillars and looked down the street. His own property filled the block on one side, and on the opposite side there was a grove. Looking on toward the Square, he could see the vague outlines of three houses a good deal like his own, old, simple in design, well placed and beautiful. The present occupants or their older relatives had been his neighbors all his life, but for many years he had entered their doors only on special occasions, such as funerals or large parties from which he could not escape.

At present the houses were occupied entirely by ladies. In the nearest lived three Misses Walter, thirty years old and a little above and a little below. All were pretty, all were bright, all were growing somewhat wistful, as pretty girls are apt to do in small towns where the male population is mysteriously absent or mysteriously unattractive. Opposite them lived Mrs. Lupton, with whom he had attended public school, and who was almost his own age. The Walter girls had no occupation except housekeeping, but Mrs. Lupton was devoted to gardening in which she was expert.

On the same side of the street with the Walter sisters lived Mrs. Corbin, the widow of one of Lucien's contemporaries; she, like the Walters, was thirty or a little above or a little below. The citizens

of Bon Air wondered why she did not go away, back
to New England from whence she came. Like the
Walters she was bright and pretty and talkative, but
she was not in the least wistful.

When Lucien looked toward the Square, he was
looking not at the houses of these ladies but through
them, through the Square, and far away to the abode
of the Youngs. He was homesick to see the Youngs,
and, though he had called upon them last evening,
there was no reason why he should not call upon
them again. But his heart was too sore and resentful; he saw Mamma's eyes beaming at Obenchain, he
heard Marian's voice praising Obenchain.

'If a man is even ordinarily presentable and has
brains, I don't care what race he belongs to,' Marian
announced coolly, and in Lucien's humble mind the
sharp words bred a sad uneasiness. 'But brains he
must have.'

Having made twenty enumerated trips from the
house to the gate, Lucien ascended the steps of the
porch and sat down. The exertion made him gasp;
he would go inside and try again to read. Johnson
and Millie, his servants, had departed to their cabin,
the house was empty; he could get into light attire
and make himself as comfortable as possible in the
coolest room.

No sooner had he arrived at this determination
than he abandoned it. The Youngs were the candle
and he the moth, and it was better to go now than
an hour later. He walked briskly down the path and

out to the pavement. He passed the house of Mrs. Lupton — he could see her white shape on the porch, too far away and too dim to make a salutation necessary. He could hear the voices of the Misses Walter which were all a little shrill. Their voices hushed; they and the night seemed to wait. But waiting was vain; Lucien passed their gate swiftly. He could see ahead the figure of Mrs. Corbin on her porch, also in white. She sat well forward, as though to catch what breeze there might be. If she saw him, she made no sign; her rocking-chair continued to sway back and forth. The air seemed suddenly to become even heavier — it may have been that the sorrowful meditations of Mrs. Lupton and Mrs. Corbin and the three Walter ladies weighed it down.

Lucien passed through the Square under the lofty trees. The business houses were closed except the drug-store, and Bon Air was like the woodland. The faint light of a street lamp shone on the façade of the Court House and its lofty cupola, and a thrill passed through the soul of Lucien. He loved beauty, but it was the beauty which he knew from his birth. He heard a chuckling sound, then a shrill cry. An owl flew from a lofty branch and swooped past his cheek; startled, he quickened his pace.

All the porches were occupied, and children played languidly under the lights. No one would go to bed early; people dreaded the stored heat in bedrooms, uncooled for days by any breeze. They

would sit and talk or be silent, they would still be
sitting when he came back. His olive cheek flushed
— how they all watched him! How they all specu-
lated about him! Which one would he take? — he
had heard the coarse inquiry. He would take Marian! If only Marian had loosed the tight fist into
which her slender hand compressed itself, if only
Marian had turned her hand ever so little, if only
Marian's fingers had fluttered!

With quickened speed, with quickened breathing, he came at last to the brick pillars topped with
their white urns. Slipping between them he went
toward the house, walking not on the path, but
on the grass, as if to make as little sound as possible.

With his foot on the terrace, he paused. The front
of the house was like a beautiful stage-set in a
theater. Within sat the actors, Mamma in pale blue
in her sitting-room, her box of candy beside her,
Marian at her piano in her own demesne. Mamma
was motionless except for the gentle movement with
which she chewed her candy; Marian was also
motionless, her eyes studying the music spread open
on the rack. If he entered, Mamma would eat and
praise Obenchain, and Marian would play Obenchain's music. He did not wish to hear him praised,
he did not wish to hear Marian play his music, he
wished him in the bottom of the sea, he wished
Marian in his arms. He seemed to hear their voices
— 'Our good friend has again remembered my sweet

tooth, Lucien.' 'Mr. Obenchain sent me more music, Lucien. Listen!'

Resentful, angry, as though he had been shut out, he turned away and went down the brick walk without paying heed to his steps. How he walked made no difference — Marian's hands were creating a loud, chaotic jumble of sounds. He strode out between the pillars and went his way toward home. The pavement was brick; ever and anon, struck with vigor, it rang under his heel. He crossed the wooded Square without looking up at the lofty cupola; he entered upon his own street; he came by and by to the region of scattered houses where he lived. At the gate he saw a white figure.

Mrs. Corbin also had been walking up and down, up and down — for her, too, the years were passing and Lucien's house was less desolate than hers. 'One more turn!' said she with a sigh. 'Then I'll go in and go ——' She caught her sigh between her pretty teeth — Lucien Clement coming home at this early hour! She was at this instant turning at her gate. 'Good-evening, Mr. Clement!' said she lightly.

Lucien stopped short. Bessie Walter was patrolling the pavement outside the Walter gate, Allie was patrolling inside the gate, Irene was sitting on the porch. All heard the sharp stroke of Lucien's heel, all made the same astonished comment — Lucien Clement coming home already!

Lucien looked down, Mrs. Corbin looked up. Her

black eyes sparkled and so did her white teeth. She had a short upper lip, a low sweet voice.

'Do come in! I was just about to have something cold to drink to make me comfortable for a few minutes at least. You, too, shall be comfortable for a few minutes.'

She spoke calmly, naturally, as though Lucien were a frequent visitor to her house — not as though he had a thousand times passed her by. She was forgiving, she was kind, she was comfortable; Lucien might do far worse than select her for his bride. He stepped inside her gate, approached her porch, sat down. Unvoiced exclamations seemed to float upon the air — 'What!' gasped Irene; 'What!' cried Bessie; 'What!' exclaimed Allie, each in her own heart.

'For a few minutes,' he consented uneasily. 'I have business matters to attend to before I sleep. I walked out for a little air.'

'And found none!' laughed Mrs. Corbin. She entered the hall and gave an order. Poor Corbin had left her prosperous; she had servants and ample means. She returned and sat down.

'I have a fad which may amuse you,' said she. 'I've always been interested in moths, and I walked out to the gate to see what was fluttering round under the light.'

Lucien was surprised — he would not have expected Mrs. Corbin to have an interest even so intellectual as moths. She did not require answers; she went on in pleasant monologue. Presently she abandoned entomology for history and literature; she spoke intelligently of Jefferson, of Washington, even of Disraeli. Her discourse enlivened the night; it seemed to change deadness into life, to create a breeze. Her lemonade continued the consoling work. Lucien felt his uneasiness vanishing and he stayed for almost an hour.

Mrs. Corbin made no protest against his departure, but rose and accompanied him to the gate. She did not invite him to come again — she saw that Allie Walter had joined Bessie on the pavement and that Irene had descended from the porch to the inner path.

'I'll stay here and continue my watch for a Luna,' said she in clear, distinct tones. 'Good-night.'

Lucien stepped on. Two white figures formed a barrier.

'Good-evening, Mr. Clement.' Younger than he, the Walters addressed him with formality. Their voices were not soft like Mrs. Corbin's, and even these few words showed nervousness and excitement. Another white-clad figure joined them, hastening through the gateway. 'It's very hot, isn't it?'

'Indeed it is!' agreed Lucien, preparing to move on. 'It is, indeed.'

They made no effort to keep him with them; their address seemed merely a reminder, a calling of his attention to themselves — the Walter family had with his family an ancient friendship, far more ancient than his friendship with the female Youngs.

He proceeded into his house — dark it was, the air oppressive. Uneasiness returned to his heart; he wished that he had not accepted Mrs. Corbin's invitation — it might bring upon him embarrassing consequences. He wondered whether it would be well to call briefly upon the Misses Walter also, and Mrs. Lupton.

Undressing, he lay down upon a couch in his bedroom. Trees shaded his roof; he seemed to lie within a dark dome under whose edges a few stars glittered. His heart turned with yearning to the dear house which was more his home than this. How foolish to be angry! At this hour Mamma still sat eating her candy, Marian sat playing her Debussy, her Palmgren, her Juon, her dear knows what madman. He wished that he were eating candy with Mamma, destructive to digestive peace though candy was, or listening to Juon.

After a while, lying on his back, he fell asleep and dreamed a distressing dream. He was a sailor, shipwrecked, not on an island, but on a mere rock, and round and round swam vague, large-eyed monsters, dressed in white. His terror was so sharp that it woke him and lifted him to his feet. He began to pace up and down his room, as he had paced up and down his yard. Now his step was not that of uncertainty, it was that of determination.

'To-morrow evening,' said he in a loud tone, as

though to hearten and encourage himself, 'I shall ask Marian Young to marry me.'

II

It was Wednesday evening and Lucien walked up and down his brick walk, his head bent. The heat, more intense than that of yesterday, was oppressive enough to bend the human head, but Lucien's head was bent, not in exhaustion but in studious thought. He was not courting sleep by exercise, he was composing his address to Marian. Marian was exacting with others as well as with herself; she required a nice adjustment of all the parts of speech; one could not go to her lightly and unprepared.

Lucien's yard was a place of enchantment. It was not open as was the Young property; unless the passer-by got a glimpse between the box pillars, he saw only the green hedge and the tops of lofty trees and the roof and chimneys. Protected on the north and west by taller more hardy oaks and hickories, several varieties of magnolia flourished, and in a sheltered, sunny corner bloomed the only crape myrtle which could be made to grow in Bon Air. Though the heat was intense, there had been no drought, and all was in luxuriant growth. Tender plants wilted in the sun, but when the sun sank, they lifted their heads.

'My dear Marian' — Lucien's heart beat rapidly, choking his well-nigh inarticulate remarks — 'My dear, dear Marian, for many years' — he smelled the jessamine and caught his breath. 'My dear Marian, the time has come when I can no longer postpone' — this was a good start, but he lost the thread of his argument. 'My dear Marian, you shall want for nothing. I have more than I can spend. Your mother and sister shall be my care.' 'My dear Marian ——'

He suddenly determined that he would make no speech at all. He would get his car and drive to the Young gate and go up the path. Without summoning Celeste, he would walk boldly in, past Mamma with her solitaire, directly to the drawing-room. 'Marian,' he would say in a loud tone, so that there might be no mistake, 'come with me for a drive.' Happily, plump Mamma could not be one of three on the front seat of an automobile. Alone, with eavesdropping and interruption impossible, he might trust to the impulse of the moment. 'Marian, darling, I have waited long!'

Intending to close the front door, he returned briskly to the porch. His car was not in his garage behind the house, but at the garage of his mechanic a few blocks away. The minor repairs were finished; he would walk thither. He locked the house door and ran down the steps. The Court House clock began to strike — could it be already nine? Mamma would say, 'Too late for my child, Lucien!' — and though Marian was twenty-one, she would yield obediently. He walked more rapidly; he almost ran, as though in a few moments that at which he aimed might be beyond his reach.

Hurrying, watching his step on the brick walk so that he might make the better time, he heard close at hand a woman's voice, shrill, amused, not a little excited.

'Careful! There'll be a collision!'

'Beware!' warned another with a little shriek.

'The limited express,' announced a third in no less agitation.

He came to a halt with an awkward and perilous slide of both feet. White figures filled his gateway; massed together they seemed innumerable, though there were only three in all. He had given his neighbors an inch, they were about to take an ell. For years he had passed by all the ladies on his block; last evening's call had been a sorrowful mistake.

'We waited till we were sure you wouldn't be going out,' explained Allie Walter loudly.

Lucien was not certain that this was Allie; the three had come to look exactly alike to him, though one had brown eyes and two blue, and one was dark and two were fair. Otherwise there was little to distinguish one from the other; they were born of the same parents, had lived in the same house, and shared the same experiences. Of the three Allie, who was oldest, was the stoutest of heart, the strongest of will. She was the strongest also in feeling — she looked down upon Bessie and Irene, she hated Mamma and Marian and even Arietta Lee with all her might. It was she who had dark eyes and brown hair. Her eyes snapped when she thought of Mamma and Marian and little Lee.

'It's nine o'clock and after,' said Irene coyly. 'Too late for little boys to be at large.'

'We wish to consult you about some business,' explained Bessie. 'We feel that some of the securities left us by our father are no longer the best for unprotected women, and we would like to change.'

'Your father was our father's business adviser,' continued Irene sentimentally. 'We felt it would be rude to go to any one else.'

'We felt that our dear father would wish us to consult you,' said Bessie romantically.

'Are you sure you have the time to give us?' Allie's tone was hard; she realized that Lucien had not answered.

'Oh, yes!' answered Lucien quickly. 'Come to the porch where we can be comfortable.'

He led the way, walking beside Bessie. He placed chairs for his guests, he sat down himself. He crossed one knee over the other. His hands appeared to be clasped lightly; in reality their grip, the one upon the other, was strong. 'Marian, I ——' He almost said the words aloud; terrified, he set a watch upon his tongue.

'Now just what securities are they?' he inquired. 'Stocks or bonds?'

Irene, Bessie, Allie — all laughed lightly and a little foolishly.

'We shall have to make a list,' answered Bessie.

'Or get them from the safe and show them to you,' said Irene.

'Are they in your house or in the bank?' asked Lucien.

'In the bank. We wished merely to talk the matter over in a general way.' Allie looked downward, as though determined that her eyes should not be seen.

'There's no hurry.' Irene sighed, sinking more deeply into her comfortable chair.

No one took up her words, either to amplify or to answer. The light changed suddenly as the rising moon shone over the roof and down upon the pleasant yard.

'This has been a very hot day.' Uttering this opinion, Bessie also sank more deeply into her comfortable chair.

'A hot summer.' Allie, too, settled herself more comfortably. Her hands, like Lucien's hands, seemed to be lying lightly on the arms of her chair; in reality she gripped the wood as one who is determined that no human power shall loosen her grasp. After a while a little clock inside the open windows of Lucien's parlor struck the half-hour; after another while the Court House clock struck ten.

At half-past ten Allie released her gradually slackening grasp and rose. 'Shall we come to-morrow evening with our documents?' she inquired.

'To-morrow evening I shall be occupied,' said Lucien firmly.

'Then Friday evening?' asked Bessie.

'Suppose we say Friday morning in my office,' suggested Lucien, very quickly. 'I have financial reports there and all the information you'll need.'

'Very well.' Disappointed, Bessie stepped from the porch, her words a sigh, as though she were departing to return no more.

'That will be all right,' said Irene, following her. 'What a lovely night!' Her exclamation was not one of joy; it was a cry of mourning for joys which had been missed.

'We'll be there,' promised Allie. In Allie's voice was no sighing and no woe, she did not mean that this should be a last farewell. She looked at Lucien standing in the moonlight; she clenched her hands into fists; she stiffened all the muscles of her body as if in preparation for a fray. She thought again of Mamma, still so amazingly beautiful; of Marian, so talented, so self-assured, so superior; of Lee, so pretty and so young. Mamma and Marian she hated, but little Lee she envied as well as hated.

Lucien did not escort them to the gate. Uneasiness was in his heart also — apprehension of failure, of frustration, awe of Marian, uncertainty of her feeling, doubt of his own courage.

He went inside and closed the door. 'To-morrow,' he said to the darkness as though to-morrow were a creature whom he feared.

III

The front of Lucien's house was dark, the yard empty of human occupants, the brick path untrod, the gate closed and latched in the gateway. It was Thursday, and Lucien walked up and down in the yard behind the house, where, also, there was a walk running from the house to a group of low brick buildings, once garden-house, servants' house, and stable, now garden-house, servants' house, and garage. In the center of the broad yard was an unshaded plot set with vegetable beds through which ran symmetrical grass paths. To right and left at the boundaries of the property were clumps of trees, now round masses of solid black. From the servants' house came faintly the odor of Johnson's pipe, pleasant to the sense of smell in the sweet, heavy air, as the flight of black crows across a pale sunset is pleasant to the eye.

Walking away from the house, Lucien faced the east. The moon had risen; hot, red, glorious, it seemed to give out heat like the sun. The mercury was still expanding; it had climbed to-day to one hundred and six, which thus far had been the maximum of recorded heat in Bon Air. There had been two prostrations; mothers kept their children indoors and older folk exerted themselves as little as possible.

The moon looked unnatural, foreign, tropical, and Lucien beheld suddenly foreign lands, seen hitherto only in pictures of pen and brush — hot desert sands, the Pyramids, the Erechtheum, the Colosseum. What a fool he had been to stay all his years in Bon Air! It was unnecessary for him to work; he had worked long enough. With the companionship of youth, of enthusiasm, of affection, he might at last begin to live. He wanted not only Marian, he wanted life.

He had been waiting for darkness, and it was as dark now as it would be to-night. He had recently experienced a sensitiveness, late-born and foolish. He believed he heard voices behind him as he walked to the Youngs' — 'There he goes!' There were laughs. 'Which one'll he take?' — the old hateful question!

They should laugh no more. He ran up the steps to the rear porch to be sure that he had locked the door. He would be gone instantly, driving out into the alley back of the lot. He heard footsteps coming round the house — light, woman's footsteps. Who on earth could it be? Some one must be taking a short cut. He sat down on the steps because it would seem awkward to be standing.

Round the house into the red light of the moon came Mrs. Lupton. Her dress was white, but stained with earth; she wore flat heavy shoes and she carried a small trowel. She had been digging with it and its burnished surface gleamed brightly. She walked gracefully in spite of her heavy shoes, and her appearance was that of maturity of mind, of composure of spirit, of adjustment to life. Her features were well modeled; her gray eyes were well set and full of expression. With a little vanity, a little care of her body, she might be handsome.

'Lucien' — her voice was as one would expect, deep and rich.

'Yes,' said Lucien.

'Do you mean that you're really here?' Her tone was not tender, it was astonished. 'You don't often stop to enjoy the beauties of your estate.' Uninvited, she dropped down on a lower step. 'I occasionally steal in to inspect your garden. I'm glad you're at home for once. I suppose you're not going out at this late hour?'

Lucien believed that she mocked him. 'No,' he answered steadily.

'Perhaps you're in your garden sometimes when I think you're gone.'

'Perhaps I am.'

Mrs. Lupton laid down her trowel and clasped her hands round her knees. 'It's good to sit and do nothing. I work myself to death.'

'Why?' inquired Lucien.

Mrs. Lupton shrugged her handsome shoulders. She said nothing, but sat and looked at the moon.

'If you had any plans, carry them out. Don't mind me.'

'I hadn't any plans,' insisted Lucien.

The rising moon grew paler and more beautiful; a night-hawk dropped like a plummet; they saw him flash darkly across the light, he uttered his loud boom. A gentler bird cheeped sweetly. Mrs. Lupton gave an account of her gardening, enumerating new varieties of peonies, of roses, of dahlias, of delphiniums, with which she had been successful, those with which she had not. A half-hour passed.

'You ought to try gardening, Lucien. It's the one dependable resource of old age.'

'Perhaps I will.' Lucien's tone was level, carefully controlled; he suddenly hated Mrs. Lupton. Old age! He was not old!

Another half-hour passed; the clock struck ten. Never would Mamma allow Marian to go now! Mrs. Lupton rose to her feet.

'Bored?' she inquired lightly.

'No,' answered Lucien.

'Well, I am, always. To-morrow's Friday,' she said enigmatically. 'Then Saturday, then Sunday, then Monday, and so on. Isn't life exciting?'

She was gone, walking slowly as though she were tired. She returned in a moment. 'The three pussy-cats are watching,' said she. 'They don't know you're here, and if you value your reputation you'll steal in the back door unseen.

'I'm not afraid,' said Lucien absent-mindedly. To-morrow would be Friday — that was the day when Mamma said she and Lee would go to Baltimore. He saw the Young house, shaded, shuttered, silent through the long afternoon. As though another than himself were responsible for his solitary state, he grew angry. He would be opposed, defeated, no longer. His determined inhalation was audible.

'To-morrow!' said he.

IV

In the bright morning, Lucien drove from his house to his office. It was not his custom to drive — Lee was no more adverse to growing stout, and he walked religiously so many miles each day. This morning, however, he felt safer mounted than on foot; in a car one had an air of business which discouraged interruption.

The blue of his car was repeated in a darker shade in the blue of his suit; his tie was blue, and he had put into his buttonhole a blue cornflower. He was at this moment by far the handsomest man, young or old, in Bon Air, and also the least vain. His intention to offer himself to Marian Young was unchanged, though already his heart thumped against his side. At four or thereabouts she would have finished her lessons; he would go to the door then and take her away. In his mind he wrote a note for her to leave for Lee and Mamma. 'I have gone away with Lucien.' She would have gone away with Lucien more truly than they knew.

He planned, of course, no elopement; anything rash or hurried or undignified was abhorrent to his orderly soul. The engagement would be announced, there would be a quiet marriage before Obenchain came to dominate the Young household more than he did already, then he and Marian would depart to return when Bon Air's impertinent curiosity had burned itself out. How far they would go he had not determined; at one moment he thought of the Pyramids and the Colosseum, at another of the Bellevue Hotel in Baltimore.

A new impulse put vigor into his motions and strength into his determination. He was not only led on, he was forced on; and, stepping into his car, he glanced round as though an enemy pressed close behind. He saw, continually, floating now to the rear, now by his side, but never coming quite to the front, the creatures of his dream. They were mighty in bulk and strength, and he was weak and defenseless.

He forgot his vague apprehension in the pleasant familiarity of the Bon Air scene. The morning had a slight measure of freshness. Householders were sprinkling their lawns and the water suggested the coolness of a shower. He waved his hand to Judge Thrasher, he bowed formally to Mrs. LeConte. He did not like Mrs. LeConte; in the first place, she was the mother of the red-haired boy who took up so much of Marian's time; in the second, she looked at him always with a twinkling eye as though she suspected his feeling and were a little amused. After this evening she would have no cause to smile.

He parked his car at the curb before his office, and again looked back over his shoulder. Then he looked forward. Inside the window of his office sat a large

figure clad in white. He wondered suddenly and
with a recurrence of his uneasy feeling what Miss
Plumley would think of his marriage.

The odor of synthetic arbutus, inseparable from
Miss Plumley, met him at the door. His office was
not cooled by the morning air; it was as it had been
the afternoon before when he had left it, scented with
arbutus, with ink, with mustiness of old documents.

'Good-morning,' said he in a genial tone, without
looking at Miss Plumley. He walked across the
room and hung up his hat — was it possible that
Miss Plumley made no response? 'It's very warm,'
said he, in a still louder tone.

Still Miss Plumley did not answer. He sat down
at his desk, and she left her machine and came toward him. This was her usual proceeding; she carried with her his mail, opened by her. Her approach
now seemed to him in some vague way unlike her
approach on other mornings, it was more deliberate,
more solemn.

'My letters?' he inquired.

Miss Plumley laid two small handwritten sheets
before him. 'I didn't realize they were personal, or
of course I shouldn't have opened them,' she apolo-
gized stiffly.

'That's all right,' answered Lucien. 'It makes no
difference.'

Lucien bent his head to read. Miss Plumley sat
down beside him, pad and pencil in her hand. It
did, after all, make a difference.

'Dear Mr. Clement,' read Lucien, blushing. 'Is it not stupid that living so close and with so many tastes in common, we should see nothing of each other? Will you not come to dinner with me to-morrow evening at seven? It will at least be a little cooler at seven than at six.

   'I am
      'Very sincerely yours
                              'ALICE CORBIN.
   'P.S. I saw my Luna.'

'I'll answer that,' said Lucien briefly. Again he bent his head.

'Dear Lucien,' read he, blushing more hotly. 'Forgive me for my sassiness last evening. I often think of our old friendliness with pleasure, and with regret at its discontinuance. Why not come to see me?
                              'Yours
                                 THEA.'

'I'll answer that,' said Lucien.

'There has been a telephone call for you — the Misses Walter will be here at nine-thirty. Here are your other letters.' Upon Lucien's desk Miss Plumley laid a dozen large typewritten sheets with business headings. 'Shall I take the answers?'

Lucien looked past Miss Plumley at the clock — it was nine-fifteen. 'Not now,' said he with dignity. He had looked forward to the coming of the Walter sisters without pleasure; embarrassed in Miss Plumley's presence he wished now that they would come quickly and stay long.

The Walter ladies were heard before they were seen. They came along the broad pavement abreast, as though none wished to be left behind. Bessie and Irene entered the office first.

'So this is where you spend your time!' cried Bessie.

'What a darling old settle!' cried Irene.

'We're here promptly at the hour appointed,' said Allie stiffly.

'This is Miss Plumley — you know her doubt-less.'

The Walter ladies nodded — they knew Miss Plumley in a sense. They had often discussed her, questioning the social correctness of her position and the delicacy of her feeling.

'Please sit down,' invited Lucien. 'Did you bring your securities?'

The young ladies looked at one another — Irene and Bessie laughed. 'In the bank!' said they together. Together they rose. 'I'll get them!' said they in concert.

Allie was nearest the door; she sprang out and across the street. Bessie and Irene commented upon the other furnishings in Lucien's office; exhausting this subject, they took refuge in the weather. Lucien sat behind his desk, Miss Plumley sat at her machine.

'Here they are!' gasped Allie, entering. 'The Square's like a furnace!'

Lucien took the securities in his hand — they were gilt-edged, of long term, productive to the limit of safety. He gave but a glance at each; he handed them back.

'Admirable!' he commented. 'Couldn't be better.' His words had the effect of an anti-climax, pronounced as they were against the gasps of Allie. 'Don't give them up.'

Bessie uttered an hysterical laugh.

'We feel safe now,' said Allie with dignity. 'I'll take them back.' She moved to the door. 'We bid you good-morning.' Her round face took on a grim look, as though suddenly she abandoned some hope or expectation. She looked meaningly at Bessie and Irene, bidding them also give up hope and expectation if these were in their hearts. In obedience to her look they rose also. 'Run in any time, Lucien,' invited Bessie. They all went out without looking at Miss Plumley.

'You may take the answers to these business letters,' said Lucien.

He dictated slowly, mopping his brow as he spoke. He attended to the property of residents of Bon Air who had moved away, he executed or administered estates, he had a good deal of correspondence about the investment of a good many small funds. It was eleven o'clock, twelve; the mercury stood now at one hundred and eight, higher than any temperature re-

corded in Bon Air. He rose to go home to his lunch.
As he stepped into the car, he heard the telephone
ring, but he did not remain to answer. Thea! —
he had almost forgotten Mrs. Lupton's name.
Lucien! — the Walters called him Lucien. He drove
rapidly, trying to create a breeze.

As he ate his lunch, his own telephone ráng, but
this sound also he ignored. It rang again, again. He
looked fearfully toward the telephone, then toward
deaf Johnson who was waiting on him, as though
the piercing sound must reach his dulled nerves.

'I'll not be back to dinner,' he shouted in Johnson's ear when he had finished eating. 'Not —
back — to dinner!'

Johnson nodded. 'Not back to dinner. I'll tell
Millie.'

'You can lock the house and go home.'

Johnson repeated his words. 'Lock the house and
go home.'

Lucien sat down in the parlor to read the morning
paper. The shutters were closed, the house had a
musty smell; it needed the hand of a mistress. He
reflected with pleasure upon the fact that the Young
house belonged to Marian. It was more beautiful
than his own and far more beautifully situated. If
Mrs. Young became Mrs. Obenchain, she would go
away; in time Lee would marry; the situation for
him and Marian would be simple. The old house
needed repairs, paint, paper, everything. He laid
down his newspaper and sat staring into the corner

of the room. He heard a clock strike the hour — could it be three? Could he have slept?

Back in the office he signed his letters.

'You have been called on the telephone,' announced Miss Plumley. She paused. 'More than once. By women. I judge they will call again.'

'I shan't be here to answer,' said Lucien. 'I'm going out in a few minutes and I won't be back.'

Miss Plumley turned sidewise in her chair. She was very pale. 'I can't have reflections cast upon me, Mr. Clement.'

'"Reflections"?' repeated Lucien in the fashion of his deaf Johnson.

'I can't work in a place where women make themselves free. I've never been talked about.'

Lucien rose and looked at Miss Plumley. A vague conception of the emotions suppressed in her heart shaped itself in his mind. Suddenly she joined the school of white-clad figures swimming toward him.

'No one would talk about you,' he assured her earnestly. 'Believe me!' A stranger look, a bitter look, came into Miss Plumley's eye. He seized his hat. 'I'm going to raise your salary,' he announced wildly. Miss Plumley said nothing. He went out and took the blazing air on his hot face and flung himself into his car. 'My Heavens!' he muttered — a violent expression for Lucien.

He drove toward the northeast, to Halesville, where he had a client. The clouds gathered in the west, and climbed higher and higher, but he did not observe them. Now and then he shuddered, but his shudder was a protest of the mind, not of the body. Now and then he mopped his dripping brow — this was a protest of both mind and body. He attended to his business and drove homeward. He saw a coppery sky, he heard a low rumble, he saw the sun darken.

In ordinary circumstances he would have taken refuge in the first inn and waited until the climax of the tempest was past. The roads were cut through woodland; it was unwise to risk the impact of a falling tree. But he drove on swiftly. Marian was alone now, but she might be alone only a little while. Indeed, already Mamma and Lee might have returned, bringing Obenchain with them. He put on still more power, driving rapidly as though to meet the storm before it met him. The speed bred in him new emotions, of haste, of dire necessity. His imagination quickened as it had not quickened in his youth; he realized what it might be to hold in his arms a woman who loved him. His gaze was set, the wind ruffled the waves of his handsome hair, the storm broke at last with fury upon the roof of his car.

With windshield drenched by a flood which turned it opaque in spite of the device intended to keep it clear, with the roads in a few moments like streams, with the chance of striking a tree already fallen, he was compelled to drive slowly. He drove, however, no less steadily and intently. He saw Marian alone in the house, not frightened — she was never frightened; but awed, nervous, glad for the sound of the knocker. She would leap to answer it; he would not wait, he would say nothing, he would enter, he would take her instantly to his heart, they would sit down on the sofa in the hall.

Bon Air had no lights, he expected none. He made a détour and drove to the Young house without passing through the town. He parked his car, and ran through the torrent to the brick terrace. He sounded the knocker and turned the latch — it did not yield. He sounded it again; there was no answer. He shook the door. They had tricked him, they had all gone away — Marian with the others. It might be that they had an appointment to meet the red-haired boy at Obenchain's. They told him nothing, though he had loved them long. Bitterly he recalled the years of his devotion. He lifted the knocker again, dropped it. As though pursued by furies he ran down the path and drove away. He remembered his house — Johnson and Millie were careless, the rain would quickly ruin any room into which it swept.

Leaving his car in his garage, he entered his house by the rear door and stood dripping. He pressed a button — there was, of course, no electric current, he uttered a still stronger word than 'Heavens!' He removed his coat from which water trickled in a stream. The coat was new and ruined. He heard

between two crashes of thunder the sound of wind
in free course through the house. Making his way
by the flash of lightning he approached the hall. The
blast came from above. He climbed the stairs. The
windows of his own room stood open; like the room
of Lee, it was drenched. He shut the window with a
slam and another muttered word. As though the
heavens spoke in disapproval there was a roar of
thunder.

On a table beside his bed stood a candle, set there
for such an emergency as this. He lit it and changed
his shoes and stockings and his trousers. He looked
about; the wall-paper had dark spots upon it, the
bed was saturated, books on his table were wet,
articles on his bureau floated in water.

Terrified by a flash of lightning which seemed
likely to split the walls, he took his candle and
descending the stairs stood shivering in the hall. He
lost his breath and did not at once regain it. There
was another flash of lightning and instantly a ter-
rific clap of thunder. He dropped into the nearest
chair. The rain and wind abated as though to clear
the way for the next flash, the next detonation. In
that instant he heard a strange sound.

'Uh—huh!' grunted a voice without. 'Uh—huh!'

He stepped to the door and laid his hand upon the
knob. Had some drunken creature taken refuge on
the porch? He would not let him in; he was as safe
on the porch as inside.

'Uh—huh!' grunted the voice again. 'Uh—huh!'

He heard a low whine — it was not a man's voice but a woman's!

Gingerly he opened the door. A man one could leave outside in the storm, but not a woman. He lifted the candle. Bon Air had no drunken women! He needed no candle; there arrived the flash and crash for which the universe had been preparing. He saw leaning against the wall a rose-colored raincoat which he knew well, a rose-colored hat, rimmed with little streams of water as by a fringe.

'What!' he shouted.

With a single motion he set his candle on the floor and pushed open the screen-door. Just in time he caught the swaying raincoat in his arms.

'I'm dying!' whimpered a soft voice. 'They're trying to take you away. Everybody's a-g-g-ainst me. Nobody l-loves you as I l-love you. I ——'

'My darling!' he cried. 'Marian, darling!'

What the raincoat held was shorter than Marian, far more slender, far lighter.

'Who are you?' he demanded, aghast. There was another flash of lightning. The rose-colored hat fell with a loud 'plop!' to the floor; he saw yellow curls, a nose slightly upturned, a ghastly little face.

'Lee!' he cried, astounded.

He carried her within and laid her on his swan's-neck sofa in the hall. He looked frantically about, as though help might be expected from walls or ceiling.

'In the name of sense!' said he wildly.

V

Lucien stood perfectly still in the center of his
hall; before him on the sofa lay little Lee. Some step
must be taken at once, but what it should be he
could not decide. There was another crash of
thunder, and with it fell the rain, descending in full
volume with a sound like the thunder. He pressed
his hand to his cold forehead. 'Ah!' said he, and
rushed away, colliding with a chair, a table.

He returned with a glass in his hand. The lightning flashed; he knelt by the side of Lee. The lightning flashed again; he put his hand under her head,
and lifted the glass to her lips. She was not dead;
she swallowed the liquid poured slowly into her
mouth, she uttered a little moan. Lucien heard the
tap of dripping water, he felt for her slippers and
removed them. His thoughts became somewhat
ordered. The candle by the door had long since gone
out, but it could be lighted again and there were
other candles at hand. He lit one, another, another;
the hall was fairly well illuminated. Lee lay now
with her eyes open. Again he knelt down. She was
conscious and, it was to be hoped, no longer delirious
but sane. She was a lovely little creature, and, he
saw for the first time, a pathetic creature.

'Are you better?' he inquired.

'Yes,' breathed Lee faintly.

'How do you happen to be out in this fearful
storm?'

The fearful storm made itself heard once more.

Lee put out her hand; he took it instantly in his warm clasp. Poor, poor little Lee!

'I was coming to you,' she whispered. 'I was alone, they left me alone, all, all alone. All day.'

'I thought you were going to Baltimore with your mother!'

'I refused to go,' said Lee in a stronger voice. 'Marian went.' She looked earnestly, sharply, cunningly at Lucien. 'I abhor Mr. Obenchain!'

'You do!' said Lucien's lips and voice. His heart and his intonation said, 'So do I!'

'If Mamma marries Mr. Obenchain, then I'll be alone.'

'You have your sister.'

'My sister!' Lee sat up. She spread out her hands before her, she moved them up and down. 'One, two, three!' she said shrilly. 'One, two, three!' Her voice rose to a shriek. Her mockery was rude, ungrateful, yet irresistibly funny; a friend of Marian would condemn her for it, an enemy would be delighted. Even a friend, however, would be amused. 'One and two and three and four and five and six and' — Lee's voice sharpened like the whistle of a siren — 'seven and eight and nine and ——'

'Lee!' protested Lucien, angry and laughing and alarmed. 'My dear Lee!'

Lee looked at him with glazed eyes. 'Say "My darling Lee."' She swayed, she leaned far to one side, she lay down.

Frantically Lucien sought for the glass on the

floor where he had placed it. His hand touched it and knocked it over; that which it contained flowed out, scenting the air. He rose and collided again with chair and table. 'She has gone mad!' said he. He collided with the wall.

Carrying another glass, he returned to the side of Lee. Again he placed his hand under her head — even her head seemed lighter than a head should be.

'Lee!' he cried. 'Drink this.'

'You must say "My darling Lee"!'

'"My darling Lee," then! What is the matter with you?'

He pulled forward a chair and sat down. Again she put out her hand and he took it involuntarily, with a feeling of pleasure in keeping it warm. She gave him both hands; his pleasure was doubled. He was shy, unfailingly respectful toward the ladies whom he loved, he took no liberties, he did not touch even Mamma's friendly elbow.

Lee opened her eyes. 'A man came to collect a bill,' she said. 'From Baltimore. I had to fight him off.'

'What!'

'I had to fight him off,' insisted Lee. 'I got the door locked just in time. Then two women came. I was asleep and they broke in. I found them in the dining-room on hands and knees like bears. I drove them out with Mamma's pistol.'

'You drove them out!'

'I drove them out. Besides, I'm starved. I

haven't eaten anything to-day but a cantaloupe and some iced tea. I didn't eat because I loved you and I couldn't eat. There's literally nothing of me but bones. I thought I'd die before I got here. I made up my mind I'd come here as a last hope.'

'Where's Celeste?' From the large choice of subjects for thought Lucien selected food.

'Gone with her beau.'

'Didn't she prepare any meals for you?'

'I believe she did,' Lee tried to remember. 'I think I did eat a little sandwich, but that was long ago.'

'I'll get some food,' said Lucien. 'I'm hungry too. I'll get food for both of us. I'll call Millie, she's down at her house. She'll cook something hot, quickly. Then I'll take you home and stay with you till your mother and Marian get back.'

'But I'm not going home,' declared Lee.

'Not going home!'

Again Lee sat up. She was smarter than Mamma or Marian; figuratively she turned her hand palm upward, and far more than that. Whether she had heard the 'Marian' before Lucien's 'darling' no human soul would ever know. She stood up, she took a step, she sank down upon Lucien's knee, as though it were her rightful throne.

'I'm never going home,' she declared again. 'I'll not live a day with Mr. Obenchain. I'll not live with one and two and three and four and —— '

'Hush!' commanded Lucien. He must put her

back upon the couch, he must fetch Millie, he must perhaps call a doctor, he must have word waiting at the house for Mamma and Marian. But first he must quench this stream of wildness. His arms closed involuntarily — there was nothing of her — nothing. 'My poor child!' said he.

'Yes,' sighed Lee. She lifted her arms and laid them round his neck, she pressed her young lips to his cheek. 'Yes,' said she again vaguely. A moment passed, another, another. There was no sound, no motion; for Lucien the very earth ceased turning.

'Are you asleep?' he asked presently with a start.

'Yes,' said Lee.

Again flash succeeded flash, clap succeeded clap, each with dwindling intensity. From the street came sounds of reviving life, a man shouted, an automobile passed, its horn blowing. Upon Lucien flashed hideously a recollection of his dream, great white bodies swimming toward him. It seemed to him that at any moment they might swim to the windows and look in with enlarged and fishy eyes. They would never cease to swim after him.

'We can't stay forever this way,' said he with a groan.

'No?' said Lee.

'I'll go for Millie.'

'Millie?' repeated Lee. 'Who's Millie?'

Lucien uttered again his strange groan. Deliberately he bent his lips to Lee's. He was weak from hunger, he was confused, bewitched. An unnatural desire filled his heart — he thought it monstrous. He wished all the Young ladies might belong to him — Mamma, Marian, Lee — Lee most of all. He could never, he knew, give up little Lee.

Into his perplexed and frantic mind looked clear-eyed, clever Lee.

'Let's get ourselves something to eat in your kitchen,' she proposed in a whisper against his cheek. 'Let's not call Millie. Then let's get into your car and go to Madison.'

'To Madison!' But Lucien understood perfectly. Marriage in Maryland was easy; in Madison lived a 'marrying parson,' notorious, defiant, fully within his legal rights.

'To Madison,' repeated Lee, her lips still against his cheek. 'Why not? It would save so much trouble. And talk. Then it would be done.'

'At this hour?' said Lucien.

'It isn't late,' said Lee. A warm stream flowed through her body, strengthening her, invigorating her. She pressed closer to Lucien. 'I've never thought of anybody but you in all my life. I think you're perfectly wonderful. I made up my mind that I was going to kill myself if you didn't love me. I couldn't stand it. I wanted to die!'

'Not die!'

'Die,' repeated Lee.

'What would your mother say?' asked Lucien.

'Mother!' Lee spoke in Marian's voice. 'Mother

will marry Mr. Obenchain. I should worry about
Mother!'

'And your sister?'

'My sister! "One and two and three and four and
five and six and ——"'

'Hush!' ordered Lucien roughly. 'Don't repeat
that nonsense!'

Lee burst into tears. 'I'm so miserable!' she
wailed. 'I have nothing, nobody, I ——' She began
to withdraw herself from Lucien's arms.

Lucien felt her moving, he did not detain her.
What she said about Mamma was true. Her mockery of Marian also had elements of truth — set was
Marian in her ways, studious, contemptuous of any
mind not so quick as her own, composed, unre-
sponsive,   prickly.   He   remembered   Marian's
clenched hand — what was it to compare with this
soft and ardent clasp, these lips which uninvited
pressed his own? His arms caught Lee before she
had quite slipped away.

'You have no shoes,' said he savagely.

'No shoes!'

'They're on the floor, soaking wet!'

Lee's heart turned again its terrifying somersault.
'I don't need them in the car. I can go barefooted.
The Madison preacher won't know you.'

'There's a Madison preacher whom I know,' said
Lucien still roughly. 'And who knows me. That's
the only sort of preacher to go to.'

Lee's heart gave another mighty leap. 'That's

so,' she agreed. She slid from Lucien's knee and
stood up, straight, though quivering.

'Let me think!' begged Lucien distractedly. 'Let
me think!'

Lee flung out her arm — round Lucien. Thus supported, she stooped to find her slippers. She stood
first on one foot, then on the other; Lucien held her
as she swayed. What she proposed was the very
height of madness.

'Lee ——' A loud sound interrupted his re-
monstrance, his refusal; the stroke of the knocker
reverberated through the house. He turned —
against one side-light of the door pressed a face,
against the other pressed another face.

'Your mother and Marian are here,' said he, not
certain whether he were saved or lost. Lee let him
go; whimpering, she sank down on the sofa.

He stepped toward the door and opened it. Without stood not one large figure and one slender figure,
but three figures of matched and moderate size —
Lucien was about to throw the door wide open;
instead, he checked the impulse already transferred
to the muscles of his arm.

'We came ——' Bessie Walter paused; she had
looked through the side-light — alone with Lucien
Clement in his dark house was Arietta Lee!

'We'll not' — Irene also had looked through the
side-light, but she had an instant longer to collect
her thoughts — we'll not disturb you,' said she with
fine scorn.

'We came ——' Allie had still a longer moment in which to compose herself. She saw Lee sitting on the sofa. She spoke with dignity. 'We came to see whether you had suffered any damage.'

'None,' said Lucien, terrified. 'None,' said he again, his panic increasing. 'None at all,' said he once more, and sharply. With fatal stupidity he closed the door upon his neighbors. His back against it, he stood looking at Lee, the weaker at the stronger vessel. He walked toward her, eyes meanwhile piercing his back.

'What shall we do?' he demanded hoarsely.

Lee moved forward, each step accompanied by a soft squashing sound. She laid her hand upon Lucien's shoulder, she drew his arm around her, she turned him with her toward the dark dining-room. Hunger seized her; she must eat at once anything — everything. Stoutness — what did stoutness matter? She leaned upon Lucien, but her faltering progress was none the less that of victory. She looked back over her shoulder, she could see no eyes, but she knew that eyes were there.

'Come, darling,' said she, as though she were forty-one and Lucien eighteen. 'Come quickly.'

Lucien looked up, down, roundabout, into black shadows, into spaces vaguely lit by candle-light. From the distant west came a low grumble.

'Another storm!' said he.

In the darkness Lee put both her arms round him. She laughed. 'The limit, isn't it?' said she.

VI

ALEXANDER

I

ALEXANDER LECONTE sat very white and still in a large room, his violin on the floor beside him, his hands clasped between his knees. He had no visible hat and his hair should have been cut at least a week earlier. The mark on his cheek brightened and was lost in a flood of color, and brightened once again. He was thin; weeks of hard work had taken pounds from his frame which was meagerly covered at the best. He tried to keep his mind on the ordeal before him, but found it impossible. He saw his mother's deep eyes, Marian Young's long lean brown fingers, Mrs. Young in her splendor. He remembered odors, the scent of lavender water which his mother loved, the perfume of the valerian flowers on Marian's piano, the warm aromatic emanation of the woods which filled the Young house.

The room in which he sat was the almost empty drawing-room of an enormous and stately mansion. The white paneling had turned to ivory and had happily remained untouched, fresh grasscloth had been hung on the walls, there were long cream-colored net curtains at the windows. The massive gilded chandeliers with myriads of prisms were still in place, and so were the heavy brass furnishings of two marble fireplaces. At the far end of the room from where Alexander sat on a green divan was a desk, and along the wall stood three more divans upholstered in dull green. A gentle breeze swayed the curtains and now and again set a few of the prisms tinkling gently one against the other.

On the walls hung four oil paintings, alike in character, and apparently by the same hand, pictures of low-lying landscapes with wide spaces of clear or cloudy sky. They made the room seem even more airy and wide-spaced.

At the broad desk at the far end of the room sat a small, black-haired, and very busy girl. Speaking in a deep voice, she answered the telephone at her side; she wrote in a large book; she lifted cards from a card catalogue and returned them to their places. She was so far away from Alec that her motions were not distinct and if she looked at him at all, her glance was too fleeting to be detected.

When the breeze blew the curtains aside, he could look out into a shady square and see the brown tower of an old church. From without entered the steady sound of passing automobiles, the clangor of the gongs of trolley cars. He breathed a sigh for a return of silence in the world.

From within there came now and again and very faintly the sound of music. There was the deep distant thunder of a piano — he smiled as he recognized the opening chords of the least hackneyed Rachmaninoff prelude. A violin wailed faintly —

what was being played he could not tell. Then, suddenly, as though a door were opened, rang out 'Away
with complaining!' in a clear powerful soprano. He
smiled; he was back in the Bon Air church, he lifted
his bow, he heard Ellie Grossart. He smiled again
and blushed. Afterwards Ellie Grossart had put
both arms around him. She had not embraced him
— embrace was too weak a word for that ursine
grasp; she hugged him. The hug had in a queer way
amused him and pleased him immensely. He felt
like an infant when it was in progress, but like a
grown man when it was over.

He saw Marian, tall and lean and brown, standing
at the foot of the steps as he came down. His heart
had leaped — this was almost too much happiness.
He paid no attention to girls as a class, but, having
passed the Young house when Marian was practicing, he had returned to watch her and to listen as
she sat at her great piano, letting no inaccuracy pass
uncorrected. Here was a creature who was more
than merely girl! Sometime, when he knew her even
better than he knew her now, he would tell her about
Madame Grossart's hug. She would say, 'I wish
she had hugged me!'

This afternoon, if he could make the train, he was
going home, and this evening he would see Marian.
That is, he would see her if all went well. He had
anticipated this moment as the goal of years; he saw
it now either as a beginning or as a cruel end.
Marian considered him self-confident; he would tell

her to-night how terrified he had been, how uncertain of himself. Sometime, far from now, he would tell her how terrified he had been of her.

He would have his trial with Bergmann, if Bergmann ever arrived; then he would take his train and ride for five hours; then he would have supper with his mother; then he would go to see Marian. He hoped that she would close the doors as she always did when they played, so that they could talk unheard and uninterrupted. He would play his Mendelssohn and his Wieniawski to show exactly how he had played them for Bergmann. He would like to walk up and down while he talked, either in the drawing-room or in the smooth-floored grove beside the house, and he would give himself the luxury of a smoke.

Bergmann came in from his country home to hear applicants for instruction in his winter classes. He was now in the building, but he had arrived late and his schedule was delayed. Alexander wished that he might walk up and down now, in this long room. He stirred uneasily and sighed, and at the far end the little girl lifted her sleek head. Her motions reminded him of a snake, whose grace he admired.

Feeling that she disapproved of his restlessness, he sat very still. He thought of his mother's eyes — they were what every one thought of first in recalling Mrs. LeConte, brown, deep, burning, beautiful. He thought of Mrs. Young, and smiled and

said, 'Saskia smiling.' Saskia, he fancied, had more
mind than Mrs. Young. He must look up Rembrandt's life — how vast was the bulk of his ignor-
ance! He thought of Obenchain — a princely chap.
He had in his pocket at this moment a note from
Obenchain wishing him well, and inviting him to
give a concert in his house at his own terms in the
winter. He thought even of Celeste Imogene, who
had once opened the door for him wearing her red
liberty cap, and who had complimented him upon
his playing.

'De dish-washin' goes by de boa'd 'less I shets all
de do's, Mist' Alec.'

He did not think of pretty Lee or of Lucien Clem-
ent, they were outside the circle of his sympathies.
Lucien was to his thinking dull and ponderous, and
Lee was light as thistledown.

His appointment had been for ten o'clock; he had
arrived at half-past nine, and it was now half-past
ten. He remembered, looking down at his own
hands, Marian's hands, long, lean, young, absolutely certain. You didn't need to worry about
Marian; she was there on the spot, as absolutely in
time with you as the low note of a chord played altogether by yourself. Her playing had a precision and
dash which his did not always possess. Once in a
brilliant passage she had carried him to a climax
which he had never before achieved. He had made
her play it twenty times, poor girl. At the conclu-
sion he experienced a desire which made him blush;

he wished to stoop and kiss the top of her brown head. Instead he asked, 'Mind if we do it once more?' He could play the passage now with the same dash, unaccompanied.

When that for which he had waited happened, he was surprised and frightened. The black-haired girl rose and came toward him, her walk as graceful as the lifting of her head. She had a very white skin as though she lived in this palace of enchantment and never felt the heat of the sun.

'Mr. Bergmann is ready for you,' she announced. 'The first door at the end of the hall.'

Alec rose, looking not at her but through her. She smiled.

'Don't be frightened! He's mild as a lamb. You'll be all right. Hold on! You're forgetting your fiddle!'

Alec returned a half-dozen steps, stooped, and rose red-faced.

'How do you know I'll be all right?' This little soul belonged to his species of 'real creatures.'

She walked beside him down the long room. 'I have a hunch. What are you going to play?'

Alec meant to speak quietly, but his voice tricked him. 'The first movement of the Mendelssohn E minor concerto,' he announced in a tone which was not only loud but even defiant.

'Some piece!' commented the girl. 'What else?'

'The Scherzo Tarantelle.' Alec lowered his voice to a whisper.

The girl's eyes were like saucers, her face had the white of a waxy water-lily.

'Good for you! I'll tell my beads. There's the door.'

Alec made a grimace, then he proceeded down the hall. There was no time to dwell upon the girl's surprise; the knob turned instantly under his hand and he found himself in what had been the stately dining-room of the mansion. Opposite the door, above the fireplace, hung the portrait of a youth trying his bow. The shades were transparent and so were the net curtains, and a shaft of sunlight fell across the portrait. He stood staring; a moment passed, another, another. Youth, grace, fire, beauty of line, harmony of color. He remained motionless, enchanted, unconscious that he too possessed grace, fire, beauty of line, harmony of color.

'Like it?' asked a man's voice.

'Rather!' answered Alec, looking round.'

At the far end of the great room in a deep chair, upholstered, like the divans in the drawing-room, in dull green, sat a small man — Alec smiled, he had forgotten how small Bergmann was said to be. He was no taller than the sleek-haired girl, and round as a kitten.

'Like to look like that and play like that and be like that?'

'Yes,' answered Alec, short and smiling, and with a queer recollection of Ellie Grossart's arms.

'What have you brought?'

Alec lifted his head. He lifted again, and unintentionally, his voice, and made his announcement as though through a trumpet. 'The first movement of the Mendelssohn E minor concerto.'

'So?' said Bergmann quietly. 'What else?'

'Wieniawski — the Scherzo Tarantelle.'

'You aim high.' The voice was dry; the little figure seemed to sink deeper into the enveloping chair. 'Let's hear them.'

Alec looked round the room. At the far end was a grand piano, and at the grand piano sat a young man with a back held like a ruler, and a bored expression. Alec walked toward the piano and laid his case on the lid.

'I warn you that I'm likely to get up and walk about,' said Bergmann. 'I may even go out. But I'll hear you.' He rose and paced back and forth before the divan, softly on rubber soles. 'Go on! Begin!'

Alec lifted his bow. He saw Marian's long hands, he saw Obenchain's kind countenance, he saw last of all his mother's eyes. He nodded to the accompanist. Remembering all the mistakes of his last performance, he charged himself to play the first theme cleanly and the second straightforwardly and not sentimentally, and not to stumble in the long cadenza. The accompanist began perfunctorily; then, at the first stroke of Alec's bow, his playing took on color, as though brightened by an enlivening emotion. Was it interest? Alec ceased to think

of him or of Marian or of his mother or of Obenchain.

He lowered his bow, feeling that he had never
played so well, or so ill. A voice came from the green
chair. If Bergmann had departed, he had as silently
returned.

'What is your own judgment upon that performance?'

'I messed up the cadenza,' acknowledged Alec
regretfully. 'And emotion got the better of me in
the second theme. But I got a fairly good tone,' he
maintained sturdily. 'After I've worked another
five years I shall do better.'

'Play your Wieniawski.' Was there a smile in
Bergmann's voice?

Alec lifted his bow.

'Nervous?'

Alec lowered his bow; that was a matter which
had to be considered by some other part of his mind
than that which directed his hand. 'Naturally!'

'Don't be nervous,' advised Bergmann. 'That's
fatal.'

The sun which had been shining in through the
transparent shades and the cream-colored curtains
climbed behind the corner of a high roof, and the
room was shadowed. The portrait grew dim, the
boy himself seemed to step back into shadow. The
walls receded, Bergmann vanished. Alec believed
that he heard receding footsteps — had Bergmann
gone away? He smiled, not caring in the least. He

remembered a passage from a book, read to him by his mother. In the center of a sunny glade in a forest stood a beautiful girl, before her a red-coated soldier, who insanely performed a sword drill round her. 'Your strokes ought to be like that, Alec. You ought to feel that if you get one hundredth of an inch out of the way you'll cut off her head.' Ah, he wouldn't cut off her head!

The sun slipped round a chimney and shone upon him. There was the lovely romantic passage to come; like the second theme of the concerto it must be romantic, but never sentimental. He concluded with regret, he lowered his bow, he turned accidentally to the bored-looking young man. In his impassive countenance there was no change, but, catching Alec's eye, he winked violently, drawing the corner of eye and mouth together. The wink was like a thunder of applause, and far more tolerable.

Reaction came swiftly. He stood blinking. A desperate longing filled his breast for something he could not define, which had nothing to do with music. Confused, he looked about. Bergmann had not gone away; he sat on the arm of the chair, like a small gray owl on a green branch.

'Well,' demanded he sharply, 'and what do you think of that?'

'I don't know, sir.' With fumbling hands Alec placed his violin in the case and snapped it shut. He passed his hand over his brow and back over his hair. He had promised his mother he would have his hair cut and he had not kept his promise. She would laugh at him and say, 'Oh, Alexander!' but she would be disappointed none the less. He lifted the case and looked on the piano for the hat which three weeks ago he had left in Bon Air. He felt uneasy, awkward, weary.

Bergmann rose and came toward him, walking like a little child with quick, short steps.

'It was your idea to study with me?'

'That was my hope.' Alec's mouth twisted a little awry.

'What are your financial circumstances, or your father's?'

'My father isn't living. My mother teaches in a high school in a small town. She has helped me up to this time, and we have a thousand dollars toward next year's expenses. I don't wish to take a penny more from her. My idea was that if you would give me lessons you might recommend me to some pupils.'

Bergmann trotted ahead down the hall and into the long room where the sleek black head bent over the broad desk.

'Miss Cope, you will arrange two lessons a week for this young man.'

Miss Cope caught Alec's eye, and, like the bored young man with the flat back, winked at him. She took up a large card.

'What did you say your name is?' inquired Bergmann.

Alec told his name. Bergmann took the card from Miss Cope's fingers and wrote upon it.

'Miss Cope will complete the arrangements.'

Bergmann turned away. Miss Cope nodded toward the far end of the room, and one of three young women occupying the divan between the windows rose and followed him.

'He must think pretty well of you.' Miss Cope pointed with her pencil — across the card in a childish hand scrawled the letters *Pd* and a large *B*.

'What does he mean?' asked Alec stupidly.

'He means *Pd* for paid and *B* for Bergmann. He takes one pupil of that kind each year.'

'I thought I'd do some teaching!'

'Evidently he doesn't wish you to do any teaching. Better take the goods the gods provide. Now about your lesson periods.'

'Who is the boy whose picture hangs on the wall?' asked Alec.

'That was the pupil of whom Bergmann had greatest hopes.'

'Where is he?'

'Lost his left arm in the war. He could have been kept out, but he wouldn't be kept out.'

'Where is he now?'

The girl placed a pointed finger at her temple. The meaning of the gesture could not be mistaken.

'Oh, no!'

'Oh, yes! Bergmann never got over it.'

'How I'd like to do well for him!'

'We all would,' said Miss Cope shortly. 'You're not by yourself in that.'

II

Alec sat in the way-train which traveled each day from Bon Air to Baltimore in the morning and back to Bon Air in the late afternoon. He had boarded it at the junction with the road to Philadelphia. It required, in spite of having a much more powerful equipment than the bus, even more than two hours to make the journey, which included a pause at each station. The station buildings were forlorn and almost entirely deserted except for a single employee. Sometimes only a few milk cans were put off or on. In spite of its disadvantages, Alec preferred the train to the bus, because one was not forced to hear conversation.

On the dusty seat beside him lay his violin and a thick parcel of music. He had planned, and his mother had planned for him, a vacation when this mountain peak was attained. It was, after all, not a mountain peak, but only a spur a part of the way up; the steep ascent was only beginning. Already his plans were formulated for years to come and he would go to work, not after a vacation, but instantly.

First of all he would have supper with his mother and tell her each detail of his hearing with Bergmann. He would describe the long drawing-room, the paintings, the sleek-haired girl, the old tower

across the square, Bergmann himself and Bergmann's friendliness.

He would then go to see Marian and tell her that
Bergmann had accepted him and that he would be
in Bon Air until the middle of September, and that
they might play daily. That Marian might have
other plans or that she could in any way fail him did
not occur to him. When one could play great music
and had an opportunity to play it, there could be
no other plans. Marian had seemed to him from the
beginning as stable as his mother in character and as
ardent in musical matters as himself. Least of all
did he imagine for an instant any plans of Marian
which included Lucien Clement.

He untied the heavy twine with which he had
bound his music together, and lifting one of the
volumes bent his burnished head above it. But he
read no note. Bergmann had accepted him as a
pupil! Chills began to run up and down his spine.
He had finished the hard part of his apprenticeship
— his study under inferior teachers in whose work
he himself had to discriminate good from bad, his
playing in restaurants where the odors of rich food
grew intolerable, where tinkling fountains and loud
conversation drowned the sound of requested num-
bers — 'Souvenir,' 'Marchèta' — oh, hateful, hateful 'Marchèta!' — the Beethoven Minuet in G,
the — he ceased to enumerate, shaking his body as
though he were a dog ridding his coat of the water
from a bath. His worst hardships were past, and

Bergmann had accepted him as a pupil. He frowned, then he laughed. No use to try, he couldn't realize it.

The volume which he held on his knee was a collection of not too difficult compositions to be played at sight; he had bought it to present to Marian, and they would play it through this evening. There was a transcription of 'On Wings of Song'; there was a stately Goldmark Andante. He saw the long drawing-room, heard the melody rise and fall, filling the air with a beautiful melancholy. Only recently had he understood how beautiful melancholy could be. There were light and lovely compositions by Bach and Handel. He saw Marian lift her head, saw her brown eyes gleam, heard her round notes and harp-like runs. She would hardly be able to wait for him to tune his violin. If she could come to Philadelphia and study while he was there — what bliss! He saw himself sitting beside her, close beside her, at a concert, their shoulders touching, their hands clasped.

He laid Marian's volume aside and opened another — this was no place to think of Marian — and sat reading the notes. The heat was oppressive, cinders covered him, the train jerked to many stops, and jerkingly started once more; he read on oblivious to discomfort.

At last the conductor tapped him on the shoulder and he looked up startled.

'Do you read that music just as if it was printing?' he inquired curiously.

'Yes, indeed,' answered Alec. 'And I hear it at the same time.'

'My word!' The conductor shook his head, half in wonder, half in doubt. 'I just thought I'd tell you we're entering the suburbs of Bon Air.'

'Thank you, sir!'

Alec gathered his violin and his volumes and went down the aisle. There was no reason for haste; grateful for passengers, the train accommodated itself to their progress. It was now half-past five, a time of day which he consciously disliked, but he felt none of the depression which sometimes disturbed him. There were a few loiterers at the station, but he did not speak to them or even see them. Bon Air was not his home, except as long as his mother was there; it had no early associations for him. His home hitherto had consisted of one human being and one musical instrument.

When he left the junction, a pale sun was shining, its brightness mercifully dimmed by a thin haze. Now the sky was wholly overcast. Rain was imminent, not from clouds which promised thunder and lightning and speedy clearing, but from clouds which would be a long time emptying. The leaves of the trees were turning as though to resign themselves, or to welcome a long rain.

He stepped out to the street, and thence up two short blocks to the shady Square. The train was gone, and, except for the grime deposited upon him, forgotten. He quickened his stride; his mother

would have heard the train, she would be straining
ears and eyes to hear and see him.

At the side of the Square before the low row of
buildings where the lawyers had their offices, he saw
a magnificent automobile and recognized it at once
as Obenchain's. If Obenchain were in it, he would
like to tell him that his ordeal was successfully
passed, and that he would be happy to play for him.
But Obenchain was not to be seen; the occupants of
the car were two ladies, one of whom was unmistakably Mrs. Young. The other he could not see; he
took for granted it was Lee. From his office stepped
the handsome figure of Lucien Clement. He felt
again a kindly pity for Clement, who was so old,
who had lived his life in this one spot, content, pas-
sionless, dull. Clement stepped into the car, and it
rolled away, almost without sound.

Crossing the Square he went on to the little house
set far back from the street, where his mother lived.
It was a charming place, all white and blue and
green. The tiny house was white, a great over-
shadowing elm tree and the lawn were green, and on
both sides of the portico were buddleia bushes
covered with spikes of blue in which butterflies fluttered all day long. The curtains at the windows
were exactly the same shade of blue as the flowers;
with whimsical pleasure Mrs. LeConte had ex-
perimented with dyes.

Alec opened the gate and walked down the flagged
walk and under the portico, taking the last three feet

in one step. The front door opened directly into the living-room, a living-room with little resemblance to any room in the Young house, but with a charm of its own. There was a piano, there were a few chairs, a few pictures, a huge bowl of buddleia, and that was all. There was really room for nothing else.

'Mother!'

'Yes!' The answer came from near at hand.

Alec put down his music and his violin and walked through a dining-room out to a tiny porch. Mrs. LeConte sat there, husking corn for supper. She looked up over her shoulder, her great eyes seeking his face, her look that of the mother who has one beloved son and little else.

'All right?'

Alec stooped to kiss her. 'All right.'

'Absolutely?'

'Absolutely.'

Mrs. LeConte held an ear of corn in one hand, a husk in the other. 'I didn't dare meet you at the station, or even at the gate. Is it really all right?'

Alec leaned against the frame of the door looking down. He appeared thin and white and tired, and for the first time, to his mother, a grown man. His eyes gleamed.

'He listened with patience.'

'With patience!'

'Well, a little better than that. He'll give me two lessons a week, and charge nothing. He asked me whether I was rich, and I said I should have to have pupils. Apparently he doesn't wish me to have pupils.'

'He must expect that you'll do him credit.'

'I like to think so. Of course I can't take it all for absolutely nothing.'

'No,' agreed Mrs. LeConte. 'I can easily ——'

'You can easily nothing, my dear. That's settled.'

Mrs. LeConte lifted another ear of corn. 'Get your bath and we'll talk at supper.'

Alec turned back into the dining-room and climbed a narrow enclosed stairway. He had a small room all in white looking out into the green branches of the elm. On his dressing-table stood a bowl of heliotrope, on his bed lay his fresh clothes. The consciousness of his mother's devotion choked his throat, burned his eyes, almost unmanned him. He stood still, his eyes fixed on the flowers. He ought not to go away this evening; he ought to stay here, and, if he played for any one, play for her. If Mrs. Young were a different sort of person, he could take his mother with him to hear him play with Marian. He flushed crimson, feeling himself dishonest, and an ingrate. Even if Mrs. Young were different, he could not possibly take his mother with him when he went on this first evening to tell Marian and to play for her! The dilemma worried him; he saw his mother sitting alone, unoccupied. Usually she was busy from morning till night, but recently he had found her sitting with folded hands. He could not let her sit alone, but he must tell Marian.

'Alec!' called her smooth voice from the dining-room beneath. 'No dreaming!'

He began to stir about. He would bring Marian here; he was sure that she would come, she was an angel. It would not be this evening, but some other evening. His mother would make them a little supper, and they would sit round the table and talk; that is, his mother and Marian would talk. He was not a talker.

The water was deliciously hot, the soap yielded its froth abundantly, the towels had the roughness which he liked and smelled of lavender, the smooth linen felt delicious against his skin. Physical comfort was not a necessity, but it was pleasant none the less. Standing before the mirror, doing the best that could be done with his thick mop of hair, he began to whistle.

'Ready?' called his mother.

'Ready.'

He took his place at the head of the little table, if it could be said to have a head, and his mother hers at the foot. A voluminous apron had been removed; she was immaculate in a white dress, and also very pretty. Sometimes she said grace, and sometimes she did not. She would have explained that she said grace when she needed it, and that this evening she needed it badly. Said she:

'Be present at our table, Lord,
Be here and everywhere adored,
Thy mercies bless, and grant that we
May feast in Paradise with Thee.'

The candles were in place, though their light was as yet unnecessary. In the center of the table was a copper bowl, filled with nasturtiums and green leaves. The corn steamed on its platter, there was another platter of cold ham, there were hot rolls and sliced early peaches and cake.

'Hungry?'

'Starving.'

When the heat of the stove faded from Mrs. Le-Conte's face, she was very pale.

'Now from the beginning.'

'I was there promptly at nine-thirty for my appointment at ten.'

Mrs. LeConte said, 'Early for once!'

Alec described the drawing-room, the paintings, the girl at the desk. A gleam came into his mother's eyes, as though the mention of the girl pleased her.

'Was she a pretty girl?'

'Very. She had short black hair combed exactly like a boy's, and pomaded like a boy's, and very red lips. I think the color was fast. She had a deep voice. She worked like a cool, composed beaver. You would have liked her, but I grew a little afraid of her. At half-past ten she ordered me into the next room. She made eyes like saucers when I told her what I was going to play.' Alec described the music-rooms and the portrait. 'It was the most living thing, a boy full of fire and grace and music. He was standing exactly like this' — Alec rose and threw back his head and lifted an imaginary violin.

'As you do,' said Mrs. LeConte to herself. 'Did Mr. Bergmann say it looked like you?' she asked aloud.

'I wish I could think there was remote resemblance!' laughed Alec ruefully. 'The poor boy shot himself because he lost an arm in the war. The little beaver told me about it.' He went on quickly. 'Bergmann's a short man — you remember his pictures. He's littler even than his pictures. He looks like a young screech-owl, all gray and soft.'

'Did you play both your pieces?'

'Yes.'

'What did he say?'

'He asked me where the Mendelssohn was wrong, and I told him.'

'You didn't stop or anything, did you?'

'No. He just wanted to know whether I knew that I couldn't play it. Then I played the Scherzo and I thought of Bathsheba in the glade.'

'You did!' Mrs. LeConte's eyes gleamed.

'I did, madame! I played it well.'

'So!'

'So. Then we went to the front room and I enrolled my name with the pomaded maiden and he wrote Pd on my card.'

'You showed him that you were grateful?'

'He knew that.'

'Now eat,' said Mrs. LeConte with a sigh.

'I will.' Alec buttered an ear of corn. 'The pretty

miss is a student, and I had a wizard of an accompanist.'

'Did he compliment you?'

'He favored me with a solemn wink.'

'You'll know both of them, I suppose. And there
will be others.'

'There were others. There were three graces
sitting together. Unhappily I had to catch my train
and I couldn't give them more than a glance.' He
laid down the empty cob and lifted another. 'Small,'
he commented. 'But powerful good. Golden ban-
tam?'

Without answering Mrs. LeConte rose and went
into the kitchen. She returned with a box of matches
and lit the candles. The light gleamed on the nasturtiums and the platter of golden corn and on
Alec's bright hair and on her own eyes. She clasped
her hands in her lap.

'There are changes among your friends here, I understand,' she said, as though the matter were casual
and unimportant. 'Mrs. Young is to be married.'

Alec lifted his head. 'To Mr. Obenchain?'

'I believe that's the gentleman's name. He's very
opulent.'

'That's him,' said Alec. 'And very handsome, and
very generous and kind. I met him at their house.
The letter you forwarded was from him. He invited me to give a concert for which he was to pay
me anything I asked. He's a kind of prince.'

'He is a Hebrew.'

Alec lifted another ear of corn. 'Yep,' said he.

'There's been an announcement of the betrothal in the Baltimore papers, I understand.' Mrs. LeConte seemed to enjoy dwelling on Mr. Obenchain. 'That is their custom. A betrothal seems to have almost the finality of marriage. Gifts have been pouring in upon Mrs. Young, I hear, both from Mr. Obenchain and from his friends. I've heard that he has given her' — Mrs. LeConte began to count on her fingers — 'a car and a chauffeur, two cars and two chauffeurs, a house, many diamonds, an uncut emerald, a lake in Vermont, a yacht, and a German police dog puppy.'

'Whoop!' laughed Alec.

'Some of the people seemed to be amused, and others are very disapproving — they're probably envious. On the whole it seems a happy and pleasant arrangement. I dare say Mrs. Young has wished for many things she couldn't have, and this will give her everything she wants. I understood some one to say the house and furnishings are not hers, but her elder daughter's, and that her personal income is very small.'

'She has gorgeous clothes,' said Alec. 'You should have seen her the evening I was there. She was the most glorious creature I've ever beheld.'

'Prettier than her daughters?' The little gleam came again into Mrs. LeConte's eyes.

'They weren't in her class. She was pure beauty, beauty without anything to spoil it, even a mind.'

'And Mr. Obenchain will value her and not after a while hurt her?'

'Oh, he'll never hurt her! She may smother him to death in syrupy affection. Is there more corn?'

Mrs. LeConte went into the kitchen and returned.

'There's another change,' she said as she approached the table. 'Miss Marian Young has married Mr. Lucien Clement.' She set down the platter of corn and returned to her seat, her eyes upon the table, upon her chair, everywhere except upon her son. 'Mr. Clement, people think, was long an admirer of Mrs. Young. Lately he has been transferring his affections to Miss Marian. Suddenly he seemed to make up his mind, and she hers. The marriage took place away from here and without previous announcement. It might be called an elopement, if a gentleman of forty-one could be said to elope. I suppose he was relieved not to have any commotion, and the young lady liked the secrecy and thrill.'

Mrs. LeConte paused as though to hear an answer. There was no answer. She went on with a little gasp, incongruous in the flow of information, running, she said to herself, like water from a tap. She determined to look at Alec — in vain.

'I remember when I should have preferred an elopement to any other sort of matrimonial arrangement.' Her voice was now steady and deliberate and cool. 'I certainly should prefer it now.'

Alec lifted an ear of corn and buttered it. Mrs. LeConte looked at him — his bright head was bent, his eyes hidden; he was applying the butter with the utmost care.

'You mean that Marian Young who played with me has married that ancient bird?'

Mrs. LeConte achieved a little laugh, light and airy as Mrs. Young's. 'Not so ancient! Only forty-one. Was he never there when you went to play?'

Alec remembered Clement sitting in the corner. Watching, was he? Chaperoning? Afraid his preserves might be poached upon? Thumbs and fingers pressed into the soft cob. 'If I'd known — if I'd dreamed!' Alec's thoughts went stumbling, the one over the other. He recalled mention of 'Lucien' as frequent as mention of 'Mamma' and 'Lee.' He felt tricked, hounded, at bay. But he would not show that he was tricked, hounded, and at bay.

'Did you ask me a question?'

'I said was Mr. Clement never at the Youngs' when you went to play?'

'Yes, I believe he was. I never know much that's going on when I play.' He took a bite of corn, and another without stopping. He must eat this, and the meat and the roll on his plate, and the dessert, then he could get away, out of sight of his mother's eyes.

'Hark!' cried Mrs. LeConte.

The rain had begun, steadily, with the sound of finality, cheerful to those who had gardens or growing crops, but heavy on the hearts of the heavy-hearted. Mrs. LeConte rose and began to clear the table. If he cared for the girl, what a prison this little house, what bars the branches of the great encircling tree, how oppressive the pouring of the rain!

'We had three heavy thunderstorms in one evening,' said she. 'It got to be almost intolerable.'

Alec sat very straight and tall and white, the fingers of the rosy hand on his cheek pointing to his lips. 'Shall I help you?' he offered, though his mother did not like help.

'You may do it all.' Mrs. LeConte returned to her chair.

Alec took away the supper and brought the peaches and cake. He set a plate of peaches before his mother and another at his own place and passed her the cream and the cake. The cake was his favorite variety, white with a layer of cream icing, then a layer of chocolate. He set the plate on the table and stood looking at it. He could easily, putting one hand on one wall, another on the other wall, burst the little house asunder, but he could not eat peaches or cake.

'Would you think it very queer if I went for a walk?'

'Not in the least,' answered Mrs. LeConte lightly. 'I expect you're tired of noise and dust and paved streets, and the rain will refresh you. Don't stay too long, will you?'

'No,' promised Alec. 'I'm sorry about the good cake.'

'You can eat that when you come back.'

Alec walked into the little parlor.

'Your raincoat, my dear! And your rubber hat, please!'

Alec returned and got both from a cupboard. The anticipation of conversation was like the anticipation of a knife to one's flesh. But there were no more words of any sort. He went through the parlor and out the door. The entering draught extinguished the candles, and Mrs. LeConte did not light them, but sat in the dark. He went down the walk and through the gate. She waited, hoping for a loud slam, but there was no slam, only the heavy sound of the rain.

III

Alec walked out the street. It was the street upon which Lucien Clement lived; he must see with his own eyes that this monstrous thing was true. It was unthinkable, against nature. Like little Lee, he neglected to turn down the brim of his rubber hat, and it formed a heavy basin upon his head. The rain had seemed to begin with all the volume which rain could have, but it had grown still heavier. There was no relief from its violence; there was continually the sodden heavy sound of rain on thick foliage, rain on house-roofs, rain on hard earth, rain pouring in torrents from spoutings.

Like Lee, Alec stubbed his toe and fell flat; his fall bred no new determination, but only fresh bitterness. He smelled the acrid boxwood, he entered

Lucien's gateway formed by the pillars of box. He approached the house, walking on the grass. He saw the dining-room, pleasant with candle-light. Lucien sat at the head of the table and a woman at the foot. Her beloved name rushed to his lips — 'Marian! Marian!' He had repeated it a hundred times, it was the most beautiful name in the world. How — how could she? He believed if Clement had been young he could have endured it; then there would have been no lowering of herself, nothing against nature in her affection.

He had learned to know what melancholy was; he learned now the nature of anguish. He placed his hand across his heart to quiet a creature gnawing there. He compared his sufferings with the agony of birth; he wondered even whether the soil was thus tortured when an earthquake tore it asunder.

Gazing at the white-clad figure at the foot of the table he saw it rise, then the dark figure at the head. Arm-in-arm they approached the door. Perhaps in spite of the rain, they would come out to the porch. He backed away across the grass to the gateway, and from there looked over his shoulder. They stood in the lighted hall, not two figures but one.

'Disgusting!' he muttered. 'Disgusting!'

His gorge rose, he felt a physical nausea as he had felt at sight of the dessert for which he had at first been so hungry. He must flee the sight which tortured him. He walked away unsteadily but rapidly. He knew the alleys, and sought the same which Lee had traveled. He traveled backward on Lee's track, stumbling over stones, catching his feet in the long grass, stepping into deep puddles. When the weight on his head grew unbearably heavy, he tipped his forehead forward and a deluge descended to the ground, splashing his ankles.

He passed into the section of sheds and stables and across the main street, then entered the alley which bounded the property of the Youngs on the rear. More than once, when he had gone to play with Marian, he had approached the house by this pleasant grassy route. Entering the gate, he had gone up the garden path, and round to the front door.

Devoured by longing to be once again where he had been happy, as though that could restore happiness itself, he entered the gateway and went up the path toward the back of the house. He stood still regarding its dark mass. Except for a light in the kitchen, everything was black. He thought vaguely of little Lee — what had been done with her when her mother and sister went marrying? Probably Mrs. Young was going to Baltimore and Lee with her when he saw Obenchain's car in the Square. Probably Lee would live with her mother.

He was not satisfied with a view of the outside of Marian's house; it was within that he had been happy. Several volumes of his music lay on Marian's piano — he could learn whether any of the ladies were at home and, if not, then he would ask

Celeste whether he might be allowed to take them.

Celeste, he could see, was in the kitchen. He could also hear that she was in the kitchen. It had been a time of extraordinary joy and ingathering for Celeste; she sang at the top of her voice that she was the child of a king, and by a king she meant Mr. Obenchain. She had been to Baltimore with Mamma and had seen the enormous and fine house where Mamma was to live.

Alec heard her loud melody — surely she would not shout like that even if only little Lee were at home! He went round the house; both from the side and front it was perfectly dark. He stumbled across the brick terrace, found the knocker and, lifting it, let it drop. There was no answer. He could still hear the song of Celeste, but she could apparently not hear him. He applied force to the knocker, even violence. He would like to join Celeste and answer shout with shout. He had known alternations of exhaustion and excitement for weeks, and now hysteria threatened.

Celeste ran through the hall and flung open the door. There was no light, but she was afraid of neither demons nor darkness.

'In de name ob sense, is you got a telegram or a message from de dead?'

'Are the ladies at home?' asked Alec in a loud voice.

Celeste came closer to the door and peered into his face. 'What Mayor ob de town is speakin'?'

'It's Alexander LeConte, Celeste. Is any one at home?'

Celeste pondered. She had long since matched them all up — Mrs. Young and Mr. Obenchain, Miss Marian and Mr. Lucien, Miss Lee and Mr. Alec. But you never could tell. Mr. Alec had paid more attention to Miss Marian than to Miss Lee.

'One of de ladies is good's mahied to Mistah Obenchain, I calls him Mistah Goldenchain, fer dat he suah is. She gone in he golden cha'iot to Baltimo'. De odah lady, she mahied to Mistah Lucien, she gone to he house to take up de obligations ob de mahied life. De still odah lady, she gone out. But she'll suah be back fo' night sets in fo' good.'

'Then they are all out?'

'All out, durin' de presen' time.'

'Do you suppose I might come in and get some music that I left on the piano?'

'Suah! Dey ain' been no music heah since dis mahyin' an' givin' in mahiage begun. You got to take one ob dese can'les, cause de 'lectricity is off since de big sto'm. Don' know if dey evah gets it fix'.'

Celeste lit a candle on the hall table. Alec took off his raincoat and hat and laid them on a chair on the terrace and stepped in.

'You he'p yo'sef.' Celeste vanished, taking up her song once more. '"Ise de chile ob a king! Ise de chile ob a king!"' A door closed, another, the sound came very faintly.

Alec stood motionless. The house was dark, cool, forsaken, tomblike. It had a musty odor, such as old houses acquire when closed in summer for a single day. He heard the pouring of the rain, he heard the ticking of the clocks. The silence grew more deep, the ticking of the clocks louder. Suddenly the loudest of all ceased to tick, and the cessation was more startling than any sudden sound. He clasped his hands to keep from uttering a groan. Marian had told him that she wound the clocks. The clocks which Marian wound were running down!

He heard the whining of the wind in a chimney, he heard the sharp banging of a shutter. There was no one to close the draught of the chimney or to fasten the shutter back against the wall. He began to feel a pity for the beautiful old house, and also a fear of it, as though, the occupants gone, it might crash together in ruin. An inner voice bade him flee.

He must find his music before he went, and for that he would not need Celeste's light. There was no piece of furniture between the door and the piano. The volumes were heavy bound volumes and he would know them at the first touch. He stepped into the drawing-room, holding his breath as he walked. The tip of the piano was not far away; he put out his hand and felt the deep tooling on the cover of his bound Mendelssohn. He did not lift the volumes; he could not go until he had satisfied his longing to stand once more on the exact spot where he had been happy. Surely, then, the last hour would become a dream! He felt his way round — there stood a stool, there a great chair, he was past them both.

Guiding himself by means of a light touch on the polished wood, he reached the happy spot where he had stood to play. He saw Marian's dark hair, her long, slender, muscular hands. He stood thinking, recollecting, analyzing. He had had no thought of Marian as a sweetheart; he did not think of sweethearting with any one; but he had thought of her as a certain element in his life henceforward. He had thought of a thousand matters he would discuss with her, of a thousand hours together, of glances which contained as much as whole paragraphs of explanation to another.

He had been tricked; he had not known what love was like. You looked at a girl with interest because she could play the piano; you began to get acquainted with her, and presto! she was part of your soul. You thought of sitting at a concert with her hand in yours, and lo, you were thinking of your arms round her, your cheek pressed to hers. You thought of walking with her up a golden pathway — and she was gone to marry an old man!

'Gone!' he groaned aloud to help his puzzled thinking. 'Gone!'

He heard a light breath, realized that there was near him a light motion. He moved his hand and touched a cheek.

'Who is gone?' demanded a hard, clear voice.

In his bewilderment, Alec saw no light. 'Who is it?'

'Whom did you expect to find sitting here?' The tone was sharp, the inflection was that of irritation.

'But you're gone!'

'I'm not either,' declared Marian still more sharply. 'My mother's gone, my sister's gone, but I'm here. My mother's to marry Mr. Obenchain, my sister has married Mr. Clement.' Marian struck a match and lit a candle standing on the piano. She turned a pale face sidewise and up until she looked into the other pale face near her own. They stared at each other dumbly.

At last words stumbled to Alec's lips. 'You're not married, then, to that old man?'

Marian began to tremble. 'He's not old, but I'm not married. The people supposed it was I. I thought every one knew now.'

'Thank God, you're not married!' cried Alec. 'And, thank God, you never could have married that old man! Why were you sitting here in the dark?'

'I was thinking of you.' Marian's voice hardened. 'I thought you, too, had forsaken me, and I hadn't a friend left in the world. You didn't write. You didn't come.'

'I've been here only since the afternoon train.'

'Did everything go well?' Marian's voice was gentler.

'Everything went well.' Alec laughed aloud, seeing again a golden path before him. Breathing
heavily, he gazed at her. 'When I went away, you
thought of me merely as some one to play duets
with, wasn't that it?'

Startled and disturbed, Marian rose and turned
half round in the narrow space between the piano and
the bench. A more deathly paleness overspread her
face. She felt her knees weaken, her heart thump.
Into her mind entered a strange idea, new and
amazing, yet natural. 'There are rewards,' his
mother had said. Alarmed, she tried to escape both
herself and him. 'Please let me by! I don't know
what's the matter with me.'

Alec barred her way. 'I know what's the matter
with you. It's the same thing that's the matter with
me. I wasn't ready. Perhaps you aren't ready.
But we weren't asked. We'll have to face it.'

Half fascinated, half terrified, Marian stood still.
He returned to the subject upon which he had begun.

'Tell me I was crazy to believe even for an instant
that you could have loved him!' Alec dwelt upon
'him,' heaping a hundred years upon poor Lucien.

'Lee's happy!' Marian laughed an hysterical
laugh. 'She's eating everything.'

Alec seized her arm. 'You couldn't have been
happy for a day.'

'No?' said Marian, slowly.

'No!' repeated Alec. 'Your soul would have died,
your mind would have grown spongy, your fingers

would have stiffened, life' — Alec became almost violent, he lifted his voice, he waved his arm — 'life would have had no zest, no pep, no kick. Now with me, you ——' He stopped short, breathless, his body trembling.

Marian looked into his eyes; they burned like fires. She looked away; her heart began again its throbbing, her body shook. She remembered Lucien's cool hand; in a sudden access of wisdom, she knew that she might have had Lucien at the moment that he touched her. She turned her head; the bright eyes were still close to her eyes.

'You played for Bergmann?' she asked again stupidly, to postpone the moment of which she was afraid.

Alec laughed and thrust the bench aside with his knee. He tried to speak, but his voice would not obey. He sank down upon the bench; he folded his arms round her, and laid his head upon her breast.

'"Oh, cease thy singing, maiden fair!"' he begged. 'For a minute, only a minute! I can't listen! I can't think! Bergmann — who is Bergmann?'

From far away came the sound of music. '"Ise de chile ob a king!"' declared Celeste, her voice faintly heard, but rich, deep, moving. Upon the roof, through the open door, drummed the rain, unremitting, mysterious, disturbing. As in a dream Marian lifted her hand; she laughed lightly; then recklessly, quickly, effectively, she closed thumb and finger upon the candle-flame.

www.ingramcontent.com/pod-product-compliance
Lightning Source LLC
Chambersburg PA
CBHW020823260626
47169CB00003B/797